I0552811

THE SCENTED CIPHER

A NORA BLACK MIDLIFE PSYCHIC MYSTERY
BOOK 9

RENEE GEORGE

BARKSIDE OF THE MOON PRESS

The Scented Cipher

A Nora Black Midlife Psychic Mystery Book 9

Copyright © 2024 by Renee George

Publisher: Barkside of the Moon Press

PRINT ISBN: 978-1-947177-51-2

Acknowledgments

I have to thank sooo many people for this series!

First, Robbin Clubb and Robyn Peterman, my critique partners, who tirelessly poured over every chapter as I wrote the book, and gave me so much feedback. This book is amazing because of them!

Second, to the readers and my Rebels, without you all, what would be the point? I am so happy and blessed to have you guys in my corner!

Third, but not least, coffee. Thank you strong black coffee for once again being there for me through every step of the writing process. You are a wonderful gift to me and humanity.

For Robbin and Robyn

BLURB

My name is Nora Black, local shop owner and part-time psychic consultant for the local police.

When an anonymous letter in the local paper exposes my extrasensory secret, Garden Cove is plagued by a series of mysterious accidents, and I find myself drawn into a deadly game of cat and mouse.

A cunning killer has targeted me by planting scent clues to a murder he plans to commit. His clues are muddy, but the message is clear: *Catch me before I kill.*

Thankfully, I won't have to piece together the puzzle alone. With my best friends Gilly and Pippa and my sweetheart Detective Ezra Holden by my side, we'll sniff out the trail of the would-be killer.

But as the danger escalates, I'll have to rely on my unique ability to decipher the clues and outsmart my devious foe before it's too late.

CHAPTER
ONE

To the Residents of Garden Cove,

It is with a sense of great urgency and a faithful duty to our community that I pen this letter. Recent events have brought to light a matter that cannot be ignored, a matter that strikes at the heart of our town's integrity.

For too long, we have been unaware of the true nature of one of our own. Nora Black, a prominent member of our community and owner of the beloved local shop Scents and Scentsability has a secret—a secret that threatens our privacy and trust.

It has come to my attention that Ms. Black supposedly possesses a gift beyond the ordinary, a gift that allows her to plunder the deepest part of our unconscious and uncover our most intimate memories. If this revelation is true, it crosses the sacred boundaries that define our personal lives.

Without our knowledge or consent, Ms. Black has used her psychic abilities to read the thoughts and memories of *unsuspecting citizens. Her ability violates our Fourth Amendment right to privacy.*

As a community, we cannot turn a blind eye to such flagrant disregard for our privacy. It is our duty to hold Ms. Black accountable for her actions, regardless of her standing or reputation.

Let us stand together, united in our resolve to uphold the principles of trust and respect that form the foundation of our town.

With the deepest unease, A Concerned Resident

"You've got to be kidding me!" My best friend Gilly Martin threw the Garden Cove Gazette, the last printed newspaper still surviving in our area, across the floor of our shop. The pages scattered. Gilly shook a fist at the offending paper. "I demand that the Gazette apologizes for publishing this..."

"Truth," I supplied.

"It's trash," Gilly spat.

The Gazette, established in nineteen seventeen, also had an online presence and was now run by social media influencer wannabes who loved a clickable headline. Ezra had shown me the article in the "Letter to the Editor" section at five-thirty this morning when he'd brought me coffee in bed. The sight of him wearing nothing but his boxer briefs, his hair slightly disheveled in that cute way I like and holding a cup of coffee out for me had been the last bright spot of the day.

"Nora," Pippa, my other BFF and co-owner of Scents and Scentsability, said. "You can't be okay with someone outing you to the entire town."

I shrugged. "They sure picked a lousy weekend," I muttered as I stacked two boxes of Red, White, and Blue soaps and lotions onto a dolly. Memorial Weekend was in full swing, and Garden Cove had been a hubbub of activity for our annual summer festival. Local restaurants had set up food trucks on Main Street, and most of the shops, including Scents and Scentsability, had rented booths for the street fair.

Initially, the letter had freaked me out, but then Shawn Rafferty, the chief of police and my long-time ex-husband, had called me, having his own freakout. It had actually calmed me down. Dealing with someone else's crisis, even at my behest, had given me a reason to get out of my head.

"Hey," I said, trying not to sound as stressed as I felt. I gave them the same speech I'd given Shawn. "It isn't like folks haven't been whispering about me for a while now. People are going to talk. And while I can't control other people's behavior, I can control my reaction to their behavior." I gave the scattered newspaper a bland look. "I'm choosing to ignore."

"You mean shove your head in the sand." Gilly shook her head. "This isn't going away because you don't make a fuss."

"If I do make a fuss," I countered, "it's only going to draw more unwanted attention."

The door chimed, and three women walked into the store. It was a cool spring morning. One of the women wore a light lemon-yellow jacket, and the other two were wearing sweaters, one pastel purple and the other a periwinkle blue.

"Ladies," I greeted with a nod. "Good morning."

They quickly averted eye contact as they headed to the display of body scents.

Gilly leaned over and whispered to me, "And so it begins."

I gave her a quick jab with my elbow. "As long as they buy something, I don't care why they're in here."

"Can I bag that up for you?" Gilly asked loudly at Periwinkle Sweater as the young woman sidestepped closer to me.

She held a bottle of lavender and sandalwood body mist, one of my signature scents.

"We're having a buy-one-get-one free," I informed her while giving Gilly a bland look. "Grab yourself another scent or get two of the same."

"Uh, thanks," the woman said nervously. She shuffled back to grab another bottle. Her friends giggled, their glances flicking furtively between their friend and me.

Instead of going to the counter with the products, she brought them to me. "Uhm, I guess I'll take these," she said, thrusting them toward me.

"You can take them to Pippa." I pointed to my thin blonde friend. Even after having a second baby three and a half months earlier, a boy they named Jordan Paul, Jr., Pippa was still skinny as a rail. I privately pondered if it was a good idea to call their daughter JJ and their son JP. It could get confusing. But, hey, I was only the godparent, and no one had asked for my opinion.

"I was really hoping to get you," Periwinkle Sweater confided. "If that's okay." She forced the bottles into my hands before I could protest.

I played dumb. "Why me?"

"You're Nora Black, aren't you?"

I nodded. "Yep. That's me."

She took a white t-shirt from a designer hobo bag. "Can you smell this for me?"

The woman behind her had been staring a hole in my direction. When I glanced at them, they quickly averted their gazes and tried to look as if they weren't trying to see if their friend was successful in whatever shenanigans she was trying to pull off.

"I'm sorry. Sniffing clothes isn't one of the jobs I perform."

She clucked her tongue as her eyes widened. "But the newspaper..."

"See Jackie," the woman in the lemon-yellow jacket scoffed. "I told you that letter wasn't real." She nodded at me. "I'm sorry, ma'am."

"But I have to know if Tucker is cheating on me," Periwinkle Jackie insisted. "He came home last night with someone else's scent on him." She pushed the cloth up to my nose, and the scent of cheap perfume, ripe with alcohol, made me turn my head. I slapped her hand away from my face.

"Your friend's right," I told the desperate woman. "But if you suspect he's cheating, he's probably cheating."

Jackie's eyes glittered with tears. "I knew it," she seethed. "See, Loretta, I told you he was cheating. Ms. Black saw it."

"I didn't—"

She cut me off. "That son-of-a-birch tree." She was sobbing now. "I've given him the best years of my life."

I frowned. The woman couldn't have been more than twenty-one. "The best years are still ahea—"

Jackie cut me off again. "He won't get away with this." She scrunched up the t-shirt and squeezed it with both fists.

Loretta, the light-jacketed voice of reason, tried to, well, reason with her friend. She put herself between Jackie and me. "Ms. Black *didn't say* Adam was cheating."

I arched my brow as I got a good whiff of her perfume. The scent was light as if on the verge of wearing off, but it wasn't hard, with my sensitive nose, to recognize it.

"You all need to buy something or leave," Gilly stepped in. She pointed to the door. "Now."

Loretta and Jackie scurried out. Gilly could be menacing as heck when she wanted.

However, the Purple Sweater friend took four bottles of body spray to the counter: Lavender-Sandalwood, Very Berry, Mint-alyptus, and Citrus Blast. "I'll take these," she said quietly, giving me an apologetic nod.

After she checked out and left the store, Pippa and Gilly turned to stare at me.

"What?" I asked.

"Is Adam cheating?" Pippa asked.

"What she said," Gilly added.

"You both know the scent has to be tied to strong emotions." I gave them a wry look. "But yes, he's definitely cheating. And it's with her friend Loretta."

Pippa gasped as she leaned over the counter. "You saw that?"

"No." I shook my head. "Loretta was wearing the same awful dime store perfume I smelled on the t-shirt. Plus, her eagerness to stop her friend and discount any assumptions about my saying he was probably cheating, well, it was a simple matter of putting two and two together."

"To add up to infidelity," Gilly finished. Her first husband, Giovanni Rossi, had been a cheater. Luckily, her new husband loved her the way she deserved. And if, for some reason, that ever changed, I knew several ways to get rid of the body.

I shrugged. "It doesn't take a psychic." The fact that I hadn't gotten a vision from the scent on the t-shirt only meant that the cologne hadn't been memory-inducing for Adam or Loretta. Not every odor had a sentimental attachment.

"Okay," Pippa said with a flourish of her hands. "If Nora's not worried, then I'm not going to worry, at least not until this weekend is over. Portman's is doing their lunch tour in ten minutes." Pippa had joined the Garden Cove Chamber of Commerce to represent our store along with her husband Jordy's coffee shop. She'd helped organize the itinerary for the event. "Rose Palace will be coming thirty minutes later, so it will be a quick turnaround."

Rose Palace Resort is where Gilly used to work as the manager of the spa. She'd been accused of killing a security guard, who happened to be her abusive, crazy ex, and the manager ended up neck-deep in a local criminal organization. Needless to say, she quit her job and came to work at our shop. Massage therapy and aromatherapy went hand in hand. Our businesses crossed over in the best way.

"And we've got Parker's Landing, Lakeshore Resort, Gardenia Hollow Resort and Marina, and Hunter's Hillside Getaway successively," Pippa informed us—as if she hadn't already given us this information multiple times this week. "Nora, do you want to swap out the booth for the store?" She gave the Gazette a meaningful look before turning her gaze back to me. "Less traffic and all." She shrugged, but I could tell she was worried about me.

"I'll be fine," I reassured her. "How many people still

read the morning paper? And besides, most of the *traffic*," I said, using her word, "will be out-of-town tourists. They'll have no idea who I am."

"No worries," Gilly added. "We are all hands-on-deck until this shindig shuts down."

"Great." Pippa put on a cheerful face, but I could see the stress in her eyes. "Text me if you, uh, need help."

"If it gets bad, I'll call Tippy and see if she wants to trade jobs for the day." I gave Pippa a tight smile. "I'll babysit JJ and JP, and she can dazzle the crowd."

Tippy had worked in the shop when Pippa had taken maternity leave, and she'd done a great job. This weekend, she was celebrating three years of sobriety. She'd dropped out of college years ago and recently started online courses to finish her degree in psychology. She wanted to work as a drug and alcohol counselor.

Pippa, her older sister, acted more like a proud mother. Considering that their parents had cut them out of their lives, it wasn't surprising that they developed a relationship beyond siblings.

"Tippy started online summer classes last week. She's got too much homework to get done, along with everything else this weekend," Pippa said, her voice tinged with pride.

"Don't you worry," Gilly said to me. "If anyone gives you crap or gets pushy..." she clenched her fists. "I'll start naming and shaming. I know a lot of secrets in this town. It would turn a stripper blue to hear all the confessions people make to me while they're on my massage table." She let out a noise of frustration. "I wish I knew who wrote that letter. I'd give them a poke in the eye with a sharp stick."

"Let it go before you give yourself an ulcer," I told her as I tilted the supply dolly back onto its two wheels. "It's not worth it."

My bestie since kindergarten pished me with a flick of her wrist. "Luckily, I have a doctor at home who can treat me."

I smiled. Gilly had married the love of her life coming up a year ago, in June, and she was still in the honeymoon phase. Her happiness with a really good man filled my heart with joy. She deserved to be loved well, and Scott Graham did just that.

CHAPTER

TWO

As the late morning sun cast a warm glow over our booth, Ari, Gilly's daughter, and Mason, Ezra's son, were setting up the displays under the branded tarp that they'd put up for me while I had gone to get more supplies. Marco, Ari's twin, was out of town for the week playing baseball. He played for the Rasfield Rangers, and they were playing a series in Arkansas. He wouldn't be back until Monday. Gilly made all his home games, but the away games were harder, especially now that summer had kicked off.

Ari and Mason were both home for summer break from college and had been inseparable. For a hot minute, when they were in high school, I'd thought Ari might have a little crush on Mason, but it turned out she wasn't Mason's type. Wrong gender.

He'd finally come out to his dad at the end of last

year, and I'd been so proud of Ezra's reaction. He'd told Mason that he loved him, straight or gay, and he only ever wanted Mason to be happy. I hadn't been there, but I'd seen the memory the next time we'd gotten dinner from the Taco Shake Shack. It had been the meal they had been eating when Mason had nonchalantly told his dad that he was gay and had a boyfriend named Dillon.

I'm pretty sure Ezra had already known—about the gay part anyhow—but I'd given him points for not saying it.

It had been another week later before Ezra had told me about the conversation. I'd known for a while about Mason, but only because Ari had let it slip once. Even so, I hadn't told a soul. I figured the young man had a right to come out in his own time and in his own way.

And he had. Huzzah.

The tarp Pippa had ordered was a bright, sunny yellow. The "Scents and Scentsability" logo across the front was in a deep purple script, and we had three tables set up beneath it in a horseshoe configuration.

Mason's infectious laughter filled the air as I wheeled the dolly the last few feet. He'd arranged the sample-sized scent balm display with artistic flair and slapped Ari's hand away when she tried rearranging it. We were selling them for three dollars a tube as an introductory offer. Mason had been such a shy, quiet kid when I first met him, but college had brought out a different side to the young man. His energy brought a sense of excitement and creativity to our booth.

It was a Memorial Day weekend four years ago when I first met Mason. Ezra had invited me to dinner with the two of them. Shortly after we'd ordered our meal, I discovered the body of a woman in the lake, cutting our date short. He'd been a gangly teen, but I could already see the man developing. Now that he was twenty, he'd filled out a bit and looked more and more like his dad every time I saw him.

Ari, a science wizard and perfectionist, meticulously organized our products by type and scent, ensuring that each item was presented in its best light. In high school, she'd worn her hair short, and her clothes were mostly androgynous. Now, her dark brown hair was past her shoulders, and she wore a bright yellow cropped tank top and a lavender maxi skirt.

The second time she reached for Mason's area, she whipped her hand away before he could slap it and flicked his ears. Both of them dissolved in a fit of giggles.

They straightened up immediately when a customer, Barb Clarence, stopped at our booth. Barb was the pharmacy tech at Craymore's Pharmacy. The first time I'd met her, she acted like I was cooking meth because I'd asked for Pseudo-Act, my favorite antihistamine decongestant to use during allergy season. I bet she had been horrified to find out that the pharmacist she worked for at the time, Burt Adler, had been trafficking drugs out of the pharmacy. Barb had treated Leila well during her chemo, and it was the only thing that softened me toward the hard woman.

"Hi, Barb," I greeted her. "Nice day for it."

She smiled. "It sure is." Leaning over, she scanned the scent balms. "I just love your Mint-alyuptus and Lavender Sandalwood. I'll take a couple of each."

"Awesome," I told her. Ari was already dropping the balms in the bag. "That's twelve dollars."

"Wonderful." Barb dug a ten and a five out of her wallet. "Keep the change."

"Or you can have one more," I offered.

"Oh." Her eyes brightened. "I'll take a Citrus Blast."

Ari added it to the bag, and Barb was on her way.

Jasper Riley and Jessica Lyons strolled into our booth next. Jasper was a defense attorney in town, and he'd briefly represented Gilly when she had been arrested for the murder of her ex-boyfriend, and Jessica Lyons had been the prosecutor on the case. Jasper was competent, but Jessica was, by definition, a shark.

"Is it lawyers' day out?" I teased the two of them.

Jessica looked practically giddy. "Just browsing," she said. "The street fair has come off amazing." She arched her brow at me. "How are you doing?"

"Fine," I said. "How about yourself?" The way she was staring, I figured she'd seen the Gazette letter. However, if she wasn't going to mention it, then neither was I.

"Oh, good," she said, giving me a knowing look. "Well, we'll let you get back to business."

Conspiratorially, she added, "I'm sure business will be scent-sational today."

After she left, I rolled my eyes. Hard. If this was any indication of how the rest of the day was going to go, I should've swapped duties with Tippi. I could be cuddling babies right now.

Mr. Lems, the owner of the antique furniture store next to our shop, stopped by with his son, Waylon. Waylon, who made metal sculptures and lawn ornaments as a side hustle, was in his mid-forties, thin but not overly tall, and his father was just the opposite. I'd bought an optical illusion windmill from his last year, and I loved watching it go in my backyard on a windy day. Mr. Lems, on the other hand, was imposing in height and girth. He was in his late sixties and semi-retired. He only opened the furniture store during peak season and collected his social security the rest of the time. He told me once it was more profitable keeping the lights off than keeping them on.

"Good morning, Mr. Lems," I nodded to the older gentleman. He was only a little over ten years older than me, but his white hair and craggy face lines made him look like he was in his eighties, not sixties. "Sure is nice weather we're having today." I cringed as I thought about how many times I would make small talk today. I smiled at his son, who was smelling the variety of soaps on display. "Morning to you too, Waylon. You all looking for anything in particular today?"

"I bet business sure is good for you," Mr. Lems said, eyeing me like the cat who ate the canary. "Can't buy publicity like that. Or can you?"

"Dad," Waylon snapped, clearly embarrassed. "Don't mind my dad, Nora. He woke up cranky."

"It's okay," I muttered. But it really wasn't. I hoped nobody in town truly believed I would arrange to publish an anonymous letter about myself as a publicity stunt. Our store was lucrative thanks to online sales and a spa clinic we supplied year-round.

"Foul," I heard someone say as they walked by behind the Lems. "Fortune telling is the devil's work."

I grimaced, but I tried to pretend like I didn't hear. "Anyhow," I said loudly. "Can I bag you up any of those soaps?"

Mr. Lems snatched his son's arm and dragged him from the stand. Waylon cast me a sympathetic look as they left.

"Wow," Ari whispered. "That dude is totally cray-cray."

"Super cringe," Mason added.

"Very," I agreed. Mr. Lems had always been a bit cantankerous, but this was a new low. If this kept up, I was going to let the kids handle the booth without me.

Mason nudged me. "Hey, isn't that the Mayor?"

Allison Green was up for reelection, and she was milling through the crowd of locals and tourists, handing out buttons and hand fans. She had on a dressy taupe tank top and khaki slacks that were tailor-fit to her body. There was an entourage of two men and three women, all dressed nicely as well, holding buckets of the swag. When she started past our booth, she scowled at me. Uh-oh, someone hadn't liked the letter almost as much as me.

I'd met Allison several times, and she knew about my work with the police department. She only cared about results, but something told me the results weren't her priority today.

"Is it just me, or did a cold front just come in?" Ari faked a shiver.

"I'm sorry, guys." I gave her an apologetic look. "This is my fault."

"Oh, bull," she replied. "These people need to get over themselves. You slay, Aunt Nora. Don't let anyone tell you different."

"What she said," Mason agreed.

One of the men from Allison's group, a handsome guy with short blond hair, came over and handed me a button and a fan. "Vote Green," he said. "A mayor who makes a difference."

The slogan on the fan and the button was "Go Green with Green." There was a QR code on the button that you could scan for more information about her campaign. I smelled the same cologne that had been on the shirt that a group of ladies had brought into the shop for me to sniff. "You don't by chance know a Jackie and a Loretta, do you?"

He jerked his chin, surprised by my question. "Why?"

I shook my head. "Not important."

He rejoined his group, and I got a short reprieve. The next round of customers were all tourists who didn't know me from Adam, thank heavens, but several of our earlier guests kept walking by and giving me the stink eye. Ugh.

The popcorn stand next to us had a line that trailed down the street. The rhythmic mix of sharp cracks and softer puffs of popping corn against the inside of a metal kettle added to the air of excitement and celebration. The buttery scent grew stronger, mingling with the scent of my soaps. There were other aromas, like sweet cotton candy, savory hot dogs, and the faint smokiness of grilled Polish sausages, but it was the popcorn that held my focus.

A shadowy figure, the head obscured by a black hoodie pulled down over his or her forehead, sits on a chair in front of an unfinished coffee table. Even if I could see faces in my visions, which I can't, this one is covered with a matching black balaclava. There are four large stainless-steel bowls on the table surface spilling over with buttery-perfumed popcorn as the figure, wearing gloves, plucks up a puffy piece and lifts it to his or her nose. The inhalation is deep, followed by a distorted chuckle.

The memory is strangely staged, like nothing I've experienced before.

"Hickory, dickory, pop," *the person says in a voice that I instantly recognized as Christopher Walken.* "If you can't catch me, I won't stop."

A chuckle ensues before the mysterious person sets the piece of popcorn down on the rough wood surface next to two 9mm bullets.

The popping had slowed as the vision faded, each remaining pop a little louder, more deliberate, until finally, the symphony faded into a gentle crackle.

"Aunt Nora," Ari's hand rested on my shoulder. "Are you okay?"

I shook off the strange memory, pressed my temples and forced a smile. "I'm fine," I assured her as I gave the displays on the tables a once-over. "You guys do great work."

"So, we can expect a bonus?" Mason teased.

"They're in the mail," I replied.

He looked confused.

"You know," I explained. "The checks in the mail."

"Why would you mail it?" he asked, clearly confused by the reference.

Ari sighed dramatically. "It's what old people used to say when they were past due on paying a bill."

"Ahhh," he said, a glint of mischief in his eyes. "A dinosaur reference. Gotcha."

Ari nudged him with an elbow to the ribs, and he doubled over as if she knocked the wind out of him.

I shook my head and chuckled. Their friendship reminded me so much of mine and Gilly's. It had been a slow morning, but we'd had a few visitors wander past our booth, drawn in by the vibrant colors and enticing scents of our aromatherapy products. Then the buses started to arrive. And the street was flooded with tourists ready to spend their money.

We'd nearly sold out of our lotions and scent balms by noon.

"I'll go get more," Ari volunteered.

A loud pop, like a firecracker hitting a bell, cut through the noise of the crowd, and a woman shouted, "Shooter!" It hadn't sounded like any gun that I'd heard, but a throng of tourists started running, pushing, and shoving each other on the street in front of us as they desperately tried to get away from what was happening.

I grabbed Ari and Mason by the shoulders, urging them to the ground. My only concern was their safety. Our booth was situated near the alley between an empty building that used to be Dolly's Doll Emporium and Barker's Antiques.

"Stay low and get down that alley until you are on the next street, then go into the nearest building and hide," I told them, my voice steady but urgent. "Once you're safe, call Ezra."

"What about you, Aunt Nora?" Ari's eyes were wide with fear, her voice trembling.

"I'll be right behind you," I assured her, giving her a quick nod and a firm push.

Edgar Jones, the Garden Cove Central Bank manager, staggered into our booth, his face pale and eyes wild with fear. He collapsed onto the ground, stretching out a bloody arm toward me. "Help me," he rasped, his voice weak with shock. "I've been shot."

Another loud pop sent a jolt of adrenaline through me.

"Go," I repeated to the kids, my tone leaving no room for argument. "Go now."

THREE

After Mason and Ari disappeared down the alley, I crawled toward Edgar, my hands trembling slightly. He had a bloody wound on his right shoulder, and as I checked him over, I saw a jagged piece of gray metal protruding from the injury. It wasn't a bullet. It was some kind of flying shrapnel.

"What is that?" His voice was strained as he grasped at the object sticking out of his shoulder. "Get it out."

I moved his hand away from the wound. "Don't move, Edgar," I said firmly, despite the panic bubbling inside me. "Pulling it out could make it worse."

He winced and nodded, his breath coming in short, pained gasps. "Hurts like hell," he muttered, his face contorting in pain.

"I know, I know," I murmured, more to calm myself than him. "Just stay still." I fumbled for my phone, dialing 911 with trembling fingers. The streets were clearing as people sought shelter and safety, but there were no more shots.

"911, what's your emergency?" the dispatcher's voice crackled through the phone.

"There's been a possible shooting," I said quickly and quietly, in case the gunman was nearby. "A man's been injured. We're at the corner of Main and Elm, near the old Dolly's Doll Emporium. He's got a shoulder injury that's bleeding."

"Is he losing a lot of blood?" she asked.

I assessed Edgar's shoulder, and the blood was barely oozing now. Had the fragment sticking out staunched the wound? Another reason for never removing impaled objects. "It doesn't look like it."

"That's great," she said. "Keep him calm and still, if you can. Patrol cars and an ambulance have been dispatched to your location," the dispatcher said calmly and reassuringly. "I want you to stay on the phone with me until they arrive, okay?"

I nodded even though she couldn't see the gesture and said, "Yes, okay." It was comforting to have someone else's voice in my ear to drown out the fear spiral happening in my brain.

"My name is Susan," she said. "What's your name?"

"Nora Black," I answered.

"Are you in a safe place, Mrs. Black?"

I didn't correct her assumption that I was married. "I don't know," I replied honestly, glancing at Edgar's pained expression. "But I can't leave Edgar."

"Is that the name of the injured man?"

"I'm not sure if he's been..." I shook my head. She didn't need my speculation about his injury. Only facts would be helpful right now. "His name is Edgar Jones."

"The banker?" she asked incredulously, then immediately switched back to rescuer mode. "The police and an ambulance should arrive soon. Do you feel comfortable giving me more information about the events leading up to the incident?"

The street had gotten quiet, and I hadn't heard any more shots. I hoped that meant the perpetrator had left the area. "I guess so."

"Did you see the gunman?"

"No," I told her. "I didn't." I met Edgar's brown eyes. "Did you see anyone with a weapon?"

"No." He winced. "I was buying kettle corn..." His voice trailed off.

"Edgar didn't see the person either."

I could hear sirens in the distance. The sound sent a rush of relief through me, and tears blurred my vision.

"Do you know how many shots were fired?" Dispatcher Susan queried.

"I heard two cracking pops, but I'm not sure it was gunfire."

Edgar moaned. "I feel lightheaded," he complained. "Please," he begged. "I don't want to die. Please, please, don't let me die."

There hadn't been much blood loss since he'd collapsed. "Did you get hit anywhere else?"

He shook his head. "I don't think so."

"Everything okay, Mrs. Black?"

"Call me Nora," I said. "Edgar says he feels light-headed. He hasn't lost that much blood, so I'm worried something else might be going on."

"Did he hit his head?"

He had fallen to the hard asphalt. Maybe he'd hit his head on the way down. "It's possible." The sounds of sirens grew louder. I gave Edgar's forearm a gentle pat. "You're going to be okay," I told him. "Help is almost here."

He placed his hand over mine. "Thank you for staying with me." There were tears in his eyes. "Thank you for not leaving me."

I won't lie. Running had crossed my mind, but only fleetingly. "You're welcome."

"Clear," I heard a woman shout.

"Clear," a man added. "Stay vigilant."

"They're here," I told the 911 operator.

"Good," she said. "I'll stay on until they get to you."

I nodded, crawling forward and risking a quick peek at the deserted street. Uniformed officers had established a perimeter on the next block, moving with precision to secure the area so the shooter couldn't circle back. They took strategic positions on rooftops and behind vehicles, their eyes scanning for any sign of the threat.

A tactical team dressed in black, with helmets and bulletproof vests, made their way up the street. I recognized the leader instantly. It was Ezra. He was the detective in charge of special investigations, which meant he and his team handled anything that the uniformed officers couldn't. I hadn't realized active shooters were on that list. My breath caught in my throat as I resisted the urge to shout for him. If the gunman was still around, I couldn't afford to give away my location. Besides, the dispatcher would have conveyed my whereabouts. I just needed to sit tight and wait.

Ezra communicated silently, using gestures and hand signals to direct his team's movements. They fanned out, systematically clearing each booth and storefront. I knew they had to ensure it was safe for the EMTs, but the minutes it took them to work their way to us felt like hours.

When Ezra caught sight of me, his eyes widened with recognition and relief. He spoke into his radio, coordinating with the team to prioritize our location. Reese McKay, his right hand in special investigations, was right behind him. They both moved swiftly and purposefully.

"Clear left!" one officer shouted, and another echoed, "Clear right!"

Approaching cautiously with weapons drawn, they assessed the threat level. When Ezra finally reached my booth, he knelt beside me, his eyes filled with concern.

"Are you hurt?" he asked, his tone calm despite the situation.

"I'm not," I assured him. "But Edgar needs help." I gestured to the wounded man.

Reese was already on her radio, calling for the medics. "We've got a wounded civilian, need EMS at our location ASAP." She pointed to the other officers in black. "Fan out," she ordered. "Make sure no one else has been injured."

Ezra helped me to my feet as Reese dropped down beside the injured banker.

"Nora," Susan said. "Keep talking to me. Are you safe?"

I hadn't realized I still had the phone to my ear. "I'm good," I relayed. "I'm with the police."

I heard her blow out a breath. "That's great. I'll let them take it from here."

"Thank you," I said. "Thank you so much."

"My pleasure. You're in good hands now." On that note, she hung up.

Edgar moaned and tried to get up on an elbow. Having the police at hand had given him a boost of energy.

"Whoa, stay put, buddy. Help is on the way," Reese instructed. "Don't move until the paramedics look you over. Okay?"

Within minutes, the ambulance arrived, and two paramedics rushed over with a stretcher and a large medical bag. The younger of the two was named Carver, he looked to be in his late twenties. The other was Mark. He had salt and pepper hair and was in his forties or fifties. Mark had been on the job for a while. I'd run into him on a few of the cases I'd worked on, but Carver was new to me. As they tended to Edgar, Ezra stayed by my side. His hand grazed mine several times—a reassurance —while maintaining a professional demeanor.

"I tried to keep him still as possible," I told the EMTs.

Mark gave me a reassuring smile. "You did great, Ms. Black. You were heroic."

"I don't know about that," I muttered. I'm not sure I'd ever felt less like a hero. My phone vibrated in my palm. Numbly, I looked down. Gilly. Oh, gosh. The kids.

Ezra must've read something in my expression because he said, "They're safe. Mason called me from the antique shop. I sent a patrol car to get him and Ari and take them home."

I nodded with relief and answered the phone.

"Nora," Gilly hissed. "What the heck happened?"

"I'm... I'm not sure."

"Was there someone shooting a gun in the streets?" She made a choking sound. "Is Ari—?"

"She's safe," I promised. "Ezra arranged for a patrol car to take her and Mason home."

She sobbed with relief. "And you. You didn't get..."

"No, no," I assured her. "Nothing like that. I heard some—"

Ezra put his hand on my wrist and gave a slight headshake.

"I'm sorry," I told Gilly. "I can't say more until I've given the police my statement."

"Can we come out of the store?" she asked. "A handful of people ran into the shop, and we're all hunkered down in the kitchen. Pippa locked us in. Oh, Nora. I've been so afraid. I tried to call you over and over, but you didn't answer. Same with Ari."

I glanced at one of the chairs behind the display table and noticed Ari's bag was in the seat. In her panic, she'd left it behind. Good. Hesitation in a crisis could get you killed. "Ari left her backpack in the booth when she and Mason cut through the alley, and I was on the phone with 9-1-1."

"Is it safe for us to leave?"

"I'll ask." I glanced at Ezra. "Is it safe for Gilly and Pippa to exit the shop?"

His brows knitted in consternation. "They're still in there?" He posed the sentence as a question.

"Yes. They locked themselves, along with a few panicked stragglers, in the back room."

"Damn it." He shook his head. "Not about that. I'm going to have to talk with my team about what it means to clear a street and its businesses, is all. Tell them to sit tight, and I'll send someone over to help evacuate them safely."

"I heard him," Gilly said. "Nora... thank you. Thanks for getting Ari out of there."

"She was my first and only priority," I said. "Well, her and Mason."

"Why didn't you go with them?"

The paramedics were strapping Edgar onto the gurney, readying him for a trip to the hospital.

"I can't say until after I talk to Ezra, but I'll tell you all about it tonight over a thirty-two-ounce glass of wine."

She chuckled. "It's a date."

I disconnected the call and slid my phone into my pocket. My fingers ached as I flexed them. I'd been gripping the device as if it were a lifeline long enough for my hand to stiffen.

Ezra ushered me to the chair, and I moved Ari's bag before I sat down. He gestured to a dark-haired officer, Anthony Broyles, a new addition to his special unit. "Take Nora's statement, then see she gets home."

The man, who looked to be in his late thirties, medium height and build, nodded and came over. Ezra squeezed my shoulder. "If I don't see you before you leave, I'll see you tonight."

I gave him a tightlipped smile and inclined my head with a nod.

After Ezra left the area, Broyles asked, "Did you see a gunman?"

I shook my head. "It was so chaotic. There was a loud sound, like a firecracker, then another, and Edgar shouted that he'd been shot. That sent everyone on the streets running."

"No shots after that?"

I shook my head. "Honestly, I'm not sure there were any shots fired at all."

He scoffed. "What do you mean? We got a dozen 9-1-1 calls describing the situation as an active shooting." His brows dipped. "You think they all got it wrong?"

"Yes." I met his flat gaze. "I do."

"What about the guy who got shot? I suppose that didn't happen either."

"It wasn't a bullet sticking out of his arm," I informed the arrogant man. "It was a piece of metal. Stainless steel, if I had to guess."

"Found a casing," I heard Reese say. "Looks to be a nine-millimeter."

Broyles gave me a look that said, "Hah!"

I resisted the urge to roll my eyes. I'd had enough shenanigans for one day, and I was seriously regretting my decision to leave the house this morning.

Reese came around the corner, holding it with a gloved hand between her thumb and index finger. "This is strange," she said. "The casing looks shredded, and it doesn't have scorch marks on it." She scrunched her face in consternation.

"Where'd you find it?" I asked.

Broyles gave me a none-of-your-business stare. This time, there was no resistance on my part. I rolled my eyes. Hard.

"Don't be a jerk, Broyles," Reese said. "If Nora's asking questions, there's probably a damn good reason."

"Right," he said doubtfully. "Because she's psychic." He shook his head. "I can't believe anyone is desperate enough to believe that crap."

I glanced at Reese.

"It was on the ground in front of the popcorn stand." She sniffed the shell. "It's like burnt butter and gunpowder." She raised her brow at me. "Do you want to smell?"

"This is ridiculous," Broyles said.

"Shut your yap," Reese snapped. She glanced askance at me.

I nodded. "Okay. I'll see what I can see." Not every aroma triggered a vision, but I hoped this one would. If for no other reason than to wipe the smug look off Broyles' face. I got up and walked over to Reese and leaned close to the empty shell. Gunpowder, butter, and burnt popcorn.

A shadowy figure gets up from the chair, takes a piece of popcorn from the largest of the four bowls, sniffs it and flicks it off a gloved hand. He picks up two bullets from the table. There is a popcorn maker, a small version of the street fair kettle, against a gray cement wall. The sinister person drops the bullets inside and steps away.

He shakes his covered head and says, "I can't wait to see how this turns out." His voice is southern and high pitched now. Definitely not Christopher Walken. If I'm hearing correctly, and I think I am, it can only be Dolly Parton. What the heck? Is there more than one person in the popcorn room?

Another low chuckle sends a shiver down my spine. "Good luck, Nora Black. I'm just warming up." On that note, there's a loud bang, and the bottom of the kettle bursts open when the bullets overheat and explode. The shadowed figure stumbles backward, falling to the ground. The laughter that follows makes me nauseated.

Bile rose in my throat as the vision ended. "The kettle," I rasped. "Check the popcorn kettle for the other bullet."

The person in my vision had called me out by name. Was the article the reason this happened? Was some madman testing my ability? The idea of it sickened me.

Ezra came around the corner, his face registering surprise as he looked at me. "What's wrong?" he asked.

"I think this is my fault," I said wanly. "I'm the reason this happened."

FOUR

Shawn Rafferty, the chief of police and my ex-husband, paced the floor in front of the large window in his office that overlooked the lake. The view was serene, a stark contrast to the turmoil inside the room. Ezra stood by a shelf lined with Shawn's awards and family photos, his arms crossed over his chest in a posture of contained frustration. I sat on a brown leather loveseat situated across from Shawn's desk, sipping a thirty-two-ounce gulper from the Pump & Go, feeling the tension rise with each passing second.

"Start from the beginning." Shawn ran his hands over his thin, graying hair, a familiar gesture of anxiety that made me recall the nervous young man who'd taken me on my first date. He looked just as anxious now. "Talk to me like I'm stupid," he added, his flat stare daring me to respond with a snarky comeback.

I didn't take the bait. "I don't know what else you

want me to say." I'd recounted the visions three times already and was growing weary of the repetition. "There's nothing else to tell."

Shawn's brow furrowed deeply. "So let me get this straight. Christopher Walken and Dolly Parton are targeting you and your visions."

I blew out an exasperated sigh. "That's what I saw and heard," I verified. "Dolly Parton, or someone who sounded like her, said my name."

"Or your visions are broken," Shawn mused. "I find it hard to believe two Hollywood icons are playing cat and mouse with you."

"Agreed," I told him. "It's implausible, but I heard what I heard."

"Is this the first time you've heard celebrities in your scent memories?"

I nodded curtly. "Definitely."

"So either your visions are fritzing or there are two people who sound like celebrities." Ezra's irritation was audible. "Maybe impersonators."

"In Garden Cove?" Shawn questioned incredulously. "We're not Branson."

Ezra's frown deepened. "I think it's obvious these psychopaths are targeting Nora and her abilities. That damn letter in the Garden Cove Gazette has opened the door for all kinds of weirdos to stalk her."

"I understand you're concerned, Detective Holden," Shawn said, attempting to maintain calm while reminding Ezra of his authority. "I'm concerned about Nora's well-being too."

"I'm not *concerned*," Ezra countered with barely restrained insubordination. "I'm scared for Nora. This perp planned a violent event to get her attention, and they've warned her that they won't end this madness unless she finds a way to stop them." He grimaced. "That means this isn't over. Not by a long shot."

"Unless Nora's visions are wrong. I mean, come on. Walken and Dolly? It's pretty far-fetched." Shawn scoffed. "Besides, a couple of bullets thrown into a popcorn kettle is more a juvenile prank than the actions of a criminal mastermind."

"A man was hit by flying shrapnel after the bullets exploded in a kettle," I reminded him. "Edgar was lucky." One of Ezra's officers had called to report that Edgar's injury was minor, thank heavens. No arteries, nerves, or tendons had been involved. Even so... "If the metal had sliced an artery, he could've bled to death."

"You can't get blood from a turnip or a banker," Shawn muttered.

I narrowed my gaze at him.

He shook his head and waved a hand in dismissal. "This story in the Gazette has kicked up a hornet's nest. I've already fielded calls from two major news outlets and a handful of minor ones about the story. We need to find whoever did this and then quickly and quietly put this matter to bed. The Garden Cove PD doesn't need this kind of scrutiny."

"Definitely wouldn't want that," I said sincerely. The last thing I needed was more poking into the police department or my role in any of the investigations. Luckily, in all the cases where I'd assisted as a consultant, there had been enough evidence to try the assailants without involving my testimony as a psychic. As a witness and victim, that was another story.

Ezra stepped forward, his jaw tight with determination. "This had to be planned before the letter was released in the paper and online."

"I agree." I shuddered. "It's too elaborate for a spur-of-the-moment plot. We need to subpoena the Gazette and make them give up the author."

"I've already called the paper." Shawn waved his hand dismissively. "The letter arrived anonymously. They did agree to send the original letter and envelope. It arrived this afternoon for fingerprinting, but it's probably exchanged a lot of hands since landing at the Gazette. I'm not holding my breath."

"Are you saying that the person who sent the letter sent it via snail mail?" I asked, raising an eyebrow. That seemed old-fashioned in this day and age of instant communication via modern technology.

Ezra shook his head. "Old fashioned like Christopher Walken and Dolly Parton."

"Yep." Shawn nodded, leaning against his desk. "And the letter was typed and printed. No handwriting to analyze."

"So you already have the letter?" I asked with some surprise. "That was quick."

"As soon as Lila got the paper this morning and read the darn thing, I called for it. I haven't seen my wife that mad in a long time," he said with a hint of a smile on his face. Lila had faced a grueling battle with cancer, enduring exhausting rounds of chemo and radiation. Two years had passed since her first "cancer-free" diagnosis, and she'd been in remission ever since. "I called Darla Potter, one of the owners of the paper. She's a friend of Lila's. Then Darla ordered the managing editor, Carol Billingsly, to send it over. We got it about half an hour ago, so it isn't processed yet."

I didn't know Darla Potter, but Carol Billingsly, well, let's just say that I understood why the damning letter had gotten published in the first place. Carol hadn't been a fan of mine since high school. She'd been on the school newspaper and the yearbook committee, and I suspected at the time that she'd had a thing for Shawn. I hoped a boy wasn't the only reason she hadn't liked me, but high school and hormones was a dastardly duo. The few times I'd connected with her over the years, our interactions had ranged from tense and brief to nonexistent.

Ezra's eyes narrowed as he processed the information. "Anonymous or not, there aren't that many people who know the particulars of Nora's ability or what kind of consulting she does for us."

"You think it's an inside job?" I asked, feeling a knot tighten in my stomach.

He shrugged, his face grim. "I don't want to believe it, but there aren't a lot of options."

"I can't believe one of my officers would betray us." Shawn shook his head, but his expression looked less certain.

"I don't like it any more than you do, Chief," Ezra said. "But we can't ignore any possible suspect."

"Fine." Shawn sighed. "You have my complete support to follow the leads wherever they take you." He slumped in his chair. "Just keep it quiet and tread lightly. Don't make unnecessary waves if you can help it."

"Do you think the letter writer and the person who put the bullets in the popcorn kettle are the same?" I'd gotten the impression from the letter that it had been an older woman. There was something about the language that was oddly formal and old-fashioned, but the shadowy figure in my vision had seemed almost giddy, which had given me younger vibes. I frowned. "What if the letter showing up today wasn't a coincidence? What if the letter is just another part of the plan?"

"What makes you think that?" Shawn inquired.

Ezra began to pace. He ran his fingers through his hair and frowned. "Nora's right. We need to assume it's possible the popcorn sabotage was planned long before the letter was made public."

I pressed my thumb against my stomach, seeking relief from the pain and pressure churning my gut.

Ezra gave me a concerned look.

"Just a little stomach upset," I murmured, dropping my hand to my side. "I'll be fine."

Shawn's mouth thinned as he ran his hands through his hair in frustration. "Nora needs to lay low until we can sort out this PR nightmare."

I gave him a bland stare. "PR nightmare, Shawn? Really? Since when do you worry about public relations?"

His cheeks reddened. "Sorry. The mayor's been on my case since the letter this morning. When she finds out the street fair incident is tied to you as well, she's going to lose it."

Three years ago, our old mayor, Aaron Trident, had been arrested for murder and kidnapping. My smell-o-vision, as Gilly called it, had been crucial in bringing him down. Shawn, as the chief of police, had been put in the tough position of taking down his boss. I'd respected him for not shying away from the truth, especially since it involved the person who could fire him. Allison Green, the new mayor, had respected Shawn's determination as well. However, she'd cautioned him to avoid anything that might look like a scandal after Trident's lawyer leaked a story to the Stupor about the Garden Cove PD having a psychic on their payroll. The Stupor was a rag magazine with sensational headlines that rarely lined up with the story content, and the article hadn't named names. Lucky for me, it meant the speculation around the story had been short-lived.

But maybe that's where this had begun. What if this was the ex-mayor's revenge? "Do you think this could be Trident's doing?" I asked, mulling the possibility. "He leaked that the police used a psychic in his case to that trashy magazine shortly after his arrest."

Trident had taken a plea deal for a thirty-year sentence with a chance of parole in twenty. I'd been upset about the leniency, but I'd suspected the Stupor article had prompted the prosecutor to offer it. There had been enough evidence to convict the ex-mayor without my psychic smeller, but I would've been called as a witness. The district attorney had wanted to avoid a "media circus," as he'd put it, so he'd given Trident a choice: thirty with the possibility of parole or two consecutive life sentences with no hope of ever leaving prison in anything other than a casket.

"I don't see how he could be involved," Shawn responded dismissively. "I get a report every time he gets a visitor, a phone call, or a letter. Other than his attorney six months ago, Aaron Trident hasn't had any contact with the outside world. He's persona non grata, even to his own family."

"Fine." I chewed my lower lip for a moment. The incident with the bullets hadn't been a spur-of-the-moment prank. The perpetrator had been careful and calculating. No, this plan had been set into motion long before the anonymous letter in the Gazette. "I think we're going to have to look at everyone who knows what kind of consulting I do for the department and the criminals we've taken down because of my nose." Before Shawn could protest, I added, "They didn't just wake up this morning and decide to come up with this elaborate plan to get my attention. My vision of the memory was too careful and calculated to be spur-of-the-moment."

In other words, whoever targeted me today wasn't a new enemy.

Hickory, dickory, pop, the black hoodie figure that sounded like Christopher Walken had said. *If you can't catch me, I won't stop.*

They'd been biding their time, waiting for the perfect moment to put on a show for my benefit.

Good luck, Nora Black. I'm just warming up.

Remembering Dolly's sinister, albeit upbeat, promise made me shiver. Now that the first act was finished, I braced myself for the curtain to rise on an even darker second act.

FIVE

My front door was unlocked, and after the day I'd had, my heart lodged in my throat. I'd texted Gilly to meet me at my house, so *logically*, I knew she was the culprit. After all, she lived next door and had keys to my house the same as I had to hers. Ezra had to debrief his team and finish up paperwork, and I hadn't relished the idea of coming home to an empty house.

Out of an abundance of caution, I texted Gilly to see if she was indeed in the house. Better safe than sorry. She texted right back.

Waiting inside. Picked up dinner.

I choked out a laugh as relief washed over me. The sound was rather tinny and off, but I was kind of off at the moment. Raising my chin and throwing my shoulders back, I went inside. The sweet and bitter aroma of strong black coffee assuaged my unease. The sound of familiar voices—and not of the celebrity variety—drew me to the kitchen. There, at the center island, sat Gilly and Ari, both in sweats and oversized shirts. Ari's hair was still damp from a shower or bath. An open pink box of donuts lay between them, its vibrant assortment almost untouched, while two grease-stained bags from the Taco Shake Shack added to the much-needed culinary delights.

When Ari's brown eyes met mine, they brimmed with tears. She shot up from her seat and rushed toward me, her footsteps quick and desperate. Her arms clamped around me in an instant, holding on as if she might never let go. Her trembling breaths came in short, uneven gasps.

I wrapped my arms around my goddaughter, rubbing her back in slow, soothing circles. "It's okay, honey," I murmured, my voice as steady as possible despite the whirlwind of emotions racing through me. "We're okay." I glanced over at Gilly.

Her expression was a mix of worry and relief. "Thank God you're okay," she said softly, her voice barely above a whisper.

I nodded, the weight of the day's events pressing down on me. "There wasn't a shooter," I said, as much to reassure myself as her. "It was a prank." I winced at the lie, but I didn't want to alarm Ari with my own fear. "An awful, terrible prank."

"Is that what the police said?" Gilly asked.

I shook my head as I let Ari go. "Someone put a

couple of bullets into the popcorn kettle in the stand next to ours, and they blew up when they got hot."

Ari's expression was quizzical. "But what about the guy who got shot?" Her brow furrowed. "Bullets don't have any momentum when they explode."

"Explain it to me in small words," Gilly told her daughter.

Ari, who loved talking science, perked up at her mom's question. "Imagine a bullet inside a hot kettle. As the temperature increases, the gunpowder inside the bullet eventually ignites. Normally, when a bullet is fired from a gun, the ignition propels the bullet forward with a lot of force, pushing it out of the barrel at a very high speed." She used hand gestures that illustrated her description. "The barrel is the catalyst that thrusts the bullet forward. However, if a bullet explodes from heat, like in the kettle, there's no containment to give it direction, so the force detonates out in all directions instead of just one." She shrugged and dropped her hands to her sides. "So, how was the person shot?"

"Smart girl and smart question." I nodded at the taco bags. "Is that dinner?"

"Yep," Gilly quipped as she grabbed some paper plates from my cupboard. "I got twelve fried tacos with extra hot sauce."

My mouth watered like Pavlov's dog. "Perfect."

"Aunt Nora." Ari gave me an annoyed stare. She rolled her hand at me. "The gunshot."

The corner of my mouth quirked up in amusement.

Ari wasn't going to let it go without some kind of logical explanation. "It was metal shrapnel from the kettle. It broke off when the bullets exploded and hit Edgar in the shoulder. Someone who'd heard the bullets go off and saw Edgar bleeding assumed he'd been shot." I took the plate of offered tacos from my friend. "The perfect dinner after a miserable day." I gave Gilly a grateful look. "Thank you for being here."

She gave me a tightlipped smile. "I'm the one who has some thanking to do," she replied. "What you did today was so brave." Her eyes pivoted to Ari then back to me. "You kept my daughter safe."

"Thankfully, turns out there wasn't much to keep her safe from." I added hot sauce to a taco and took a bite. The heat and spice burned my lips as a brief hum of satisfaction rumbled in my throat.

Gilly came around the center island and grabbed me into a hug. I barely saved the taco I held from being trapped between us.

"You didn't know it wasn't real," she said fiercely. "Your first thought was for my kid, and I can't tell you how much I love you for it."

I set the taco down and hugged her back. "I love you too. And..." I reached over and put my hand on Ari's shoulder. "...I love my godchildren. Putting Ari's safety ahead of mine was a no-brainer." I felt the same way about Mason as well.

Abruptly, Gilly let me go and threw her hands in the

air. "What idiot thinks exploding bullets in a crowded street is funny?"

I gave a non-committal grunt to avoid answering her question.

Gilly's eyebrow shot up. "What aren't you telling me?"

I scratched my cheek and shifted my gaze to Ari then back to my friend. "Now's not the right time."

Ari sucked her teeth. "I'm not a child anymore, Aunt Nora."

"I know," I told her. Ari knew about my scent-memory gift. She'd even used her computer skills to help with a case in the past. "I had a vision. The person or persons who did this seems to want me to know that they're targeting me."

"Was it a man or a woman?" Gilly asked.

"Both, maybe. I don't know." I gave a quick head shake. There were two distinct voices, but I only saw one person. "I think my visions are glitching. He or she..."

"Or they," Ari muttered.

I inclined my head at her. "Or they." I scratched my scalp to mitigate the sensory overload in my brain. "The voice...the first vision the person sounded like Christopher Walken." I inclined my head at Ari. "He was a big actor when your mom and I were young."

She rolled her eyes. "I know who Christopher Walken is, Aunt Nora. He's that old guy that danced in Fatboy Slim's "Weapon of Choice" music video." Her eyes brightened. "And he plays the emperor in Dune. You know, the new one with Timothée Chalamet."

"Good to know he's relevant with the youth." I smirked. "Any how, his voice is really distinctive, and I had a second vision where the voice sounded like Dolly Parton."

Before I could say more, Ari jumped in. "Dolly is bussin'"

I'd been around the kids long enough to know that bussin' meant really good. "Agreed. Dolly is fire," I replied. "But in my vision, she was menacing, and she called me out by name."

"Maybe the adrenaline threw your gift out of whack," Gilly suggested.

I shook my head. "The first one happened before the fake shooting. The person wore all black, including a hoodie and a balaclava to cover their hair and face. Even the phone they held was black."

"Phone?" Ari snapped her fingers. "Maybe they were using a voice changer."

"A voice changer?" Gilly tucked her chin. "That's very film noir."

"It's an easy app to download on the phone," Ari said. "They have dozens of them, including one that will change your voice to that of a celebrity."

I felt like a dummy. "That makes the most sense."

Gilly brightened. "Is there a way to find out if someone has the app on their phone?"

I grimaced. "Not really. Not without a warrant." I

picked my taco back up. "And we need a suspect to get a warrant, along with more evidence than my scent-o-rama drama.

"It's too bad we can't record your visions," Ari said, unwrapping a taco. "I have a friend who's studying audio forensics. She could reverse engineer the voice changer to find the person's real voice."

"Mmm-hmm." I bobbed my head as I finished my bite. "It'd be nice."

Gilly sighed, running a hand through her hair. "That letter in the Gazette... it's changed everything. People are scared, and some are angry. Whoever wrote it knew exactly what they were doing."

I swallowed hard, the reality of my situation sinking in even deeper. "We need to find out who's behind this," I said, determination hardening my voice. "And what they plan to do next?"

The doorbell dinged, and the three of us froze in place momentarily.

"I'll get it," Ari volunteered.

I grabbed her arm before she could escape the kitchen. "I'm not expecting anyone."

"Ezra?" Gilly queried.

"He wouldn't ring my bell."

Gilly snickered. "That's not what I've heard.

I rolled my eyes. "You know what I mean." I cautioned Gilly and Ari to stay behind me as we walked out of the kitchen and into the living room. I cursed myself for not locking the door behind me, but I never locked my door when I was home unless I was sleeping. "It's probably safe," I said, unsure whether I was trying to convince them or myself. "I mean, bad guys don't advertise their arrival, right?"

Three loud knocks stopped me in my tracks. Gilly, who was right on my butt, bumped into me, and I careened forward, staggering my steps to keep upright. Several illicit expletives fell from my lips as I righted.

"Sorry, sorry," Gilly whispered harshly. The grimace on her face deepened her frown lines.

"This is ridiculous," I hissed back before rushing to the door and locking it. "Who's there?" I demanded of the person behind the door.

"Garden Cove Floral delivery," a guy said.

I shot Gilly a *WTF* look. Her eyes widened as her brows went up with a quick *Your guess is as good as mine* look.

Ari was peeking through the curtain. "It's Brady Newsome," she said. "I went to school with him. Besides, his van has the Garden Cove Floral logo on the side, and he's holding a bouquet of flowers. He's legit."

"Hey, Ari," the delivery guy said as he leaned to look inside the window.

My goddaughter gave him a slight wave. "Hold on," she said, then looked at me. "I think it's safe to answer the door."

I didn't know Brady from Adam, but I acquiesced. "Okay."

Gilly rubbed her hands together, her shoulders

bunching with excitement. "I wonder who the flowers are from?"

I opened the door and saw the most beautiful bouquet of vibrant fuchsia and white starfighter lilies. This flower was divisive: You either loved the scent or hated it. I'd always thought the aromatic tropical sweetness with notes of honey was heavenly, like ambrosia for the gods. "Is there a card?" I asked suspiciously.

"Yes, ma'am," Brady said. He plucked a small envelope from the center and handed it to me.

I opened it to find a card that said, *Love, EZ.*

Awww. My heart melted. After a lousy day, the flowers from my sweetheart made the awful seem not so bad.

"That's so sweet," Gilly said.

"When was the order made?" I asked Brady. "Was it today?"

He shook his head and tugged on his cap. "The order came in last week with today as the delivery date."

"Oh my gosh, Nora. Did you forget an anniversary or something?"

Had I? Our four-year dating-aversary had passed a couple months earlier, but maybe today had another significance. I wracked my brain, but I couldn't think of a thing.

"Oh," Ari exclaimed. "Maybe he's planning on proposing!"

I groaned. "Don't even joke about that." After the day I had, a proposal was the last thing I needed or wanted. I didn't want to get married ever. I'd been there, done that, and got the t-shirt in the divorce. I liked our relationship the way it was. As far as I knew, Ezra felt the same. I hoped and prayed that wasn't the reason for the flowers.

"These things were really stinking up the van." His expression soured, and he gulped. "I mean, it was just they were a lot to drive around with."

The flower was known for its strong perfume, but I thought the kid exaggerated his complaint until he jerked his thumb back to the van. "There are seven more bouquets in the back seat."

"This is serious," Gilly said with less mirth. "You don't buy eight bouquets of flowers ahead of time unless you have something big in mind."

I gave her a quick, light backhand. "Say less." The pit in my stomach grew into a deep well, and I wanted to crawl inside and hide. "I don't suppose you could take them back?" I asked Brady.

"Sorry, no." He adjusted the brim of his hat again, his blue eyes sparkling. "I think you should give the guy a chance. He must really love you."

I sighed. "Fine. You can bring them in." I lifted the bouquet to my nose and inhaled the honied fragrance. The sweet notes were pleasantly pungent until...

Someone wearing all white, including a white hoodie, gloves, and mask, stands in a white, sterile-looking room surrounded by tables and bunches of pink and white Starfighter lilies. The flowers are tucked in white buckets surrounding the figure. The sweet, pungent aroma saturates the air. Stem and leaf clippings litter the table tops and floor.

He or she walks over and sits on a stool. They are humming a song that sounds vaguely familiar. What is it from? One of the shows I grew up with as a child, I think. They have something in their hand, a can maybe, but without a label. They start wrapping something onto the exterior with duct tape.

"EZ Holden, that's his name," the melodic smooth voice sings softly. "EZ Holden will play my game."

I recognize the voice and the song. The person sounded like Morgan Freeman, and the tune was EZ Reader.

In white-gloved hands, the sinister figure holds out a metal canister with a timer attached. "Time's not your friend, Nora. It's ticking away. Will you find the bomb before it finds its prey? For someone with your gifts, it should be easy." The bomb is set onto the ground, and the Morgan Freeman chuckles. "I hope you can speed read, Hero. Tick tock. You have three hours before the clock runs out."

I dropped the bouquet, and the hard glass vase they were in bounced, sloshing water over my feet and my carpet.

"What did you see?" Gilly immediately asked. "You're white as a sheet."

"A bomb," I whispered hoarsely. "We have to find the bomb before it's too late."

SIX

I scrambled to the kitchen to retrieve my phone and immediately called Ezra. The mystery maniac had used Ezra's name to taunt me, and I worried he was the target.

He picked up on the first ring. "Hey," he answered, wind noise in the background.

"Are you driving?" I asked.

"Yeah, I wrapped things up at the station, and I'm headed to you now."

A sudden horrendous idea popped into my head. "Get off the road and get out of your truck!" If Ezra was the target, what better way to get him than to put the bomb under his vehicle?

"What's going on?"

"Just do it, Ezra. Please. There might be a bomb."

I heard the squeal of brakes, the engine cut, and the door open and close. "Hold on," he said, his voice distant. "I have to take you off the truck speakers." There was a pause, and then, much more clearly, he said, "There. I'm out. What's this about a bomb?"

"I had another vision," I started, then proceeded to tell him about the delivery of Starfighter lilies and the memory of the stranger in white, how he'd used Ezra's name in his ditty, and how he said I had three hours to find the bomb before it went off.

"Three hours?" Ezra sounded incredulous. "How could he know when you would get the vision?"

"Or she," I said.

"Almost eighty percent of violent crimes are perpetrated by men, so let's work on the assumption that this person is a guy. With a willingness to change the assumption with further evidence and facts."

"Agreed." As scared as I was for Ezra, I couldn't stop the hint of a smile tugging at my lips.

"So, three hours..."

"I don't know," I told him. I snapped at Brady to get his attention. "What were the instructions on that order?" I asked. "You said it came in a week ago?"

Brady, who had been listening with growing anxiety, paled visibly. "A bomb?" he stammered. His hands began to shake, and he looked around as if expecting the van to explode any second. "Are you serious?"

"Yes, I'm serious," I said firmly. "Now, what were the instructions on that order?"

"The flowers were to be delivered today at five o'clock sharp," he said, his voice quivering.

"It's only four-thirty," Gilly said. "He's early."

Brady winced. "The smell of the flowers made me sick to my stomach." He removed his hat and shoved it in his back pocket, revealing a thick, dark mop of hair that framed his face and made his blue eyes almost glow in contrast. "I have two other deliveries outside of town, so I decided to do this one first to get those lilies out of the van. It's not a big deal, right?" He had a hangdog expression as he rubbed his face. "Don't tell my boss. She insisted I get the order here at the precise time. The customer paid extra money for it."

I nodded at Brady and let him off the hook. "Stay put. The police will want to talk to you when they get here."

"Aw man," he groaned, visibly distressed. "I'm gonna get so fired."

I turned my attention back to my phone and Ezra. "Did you hear that? The delivery was supposed to be here at five," I told him. "But the driver got here early."

"If there's a three-hour window, whatever is going down is supposed to happen at eight o'clock."

"And we have three and a half hours to stop it."

"I'll be over soon. Hang tight, okay?"

"Don't drive your truck," I told him. "Not until you can get your bomb disposal people on it."

"I've got one guy," Ezra said. "I'll call him as soon as I hang up. I'll call Reese and have her pick me up. In the meantime, I'll get some uniforms over there to go over the van and take statements."

"Okay." I was comforted knowing he was on his way. "See you soon."

"I love you," he said as his parting words.

"Love you back." I disconnected the call.

Gilly's gaze met mine. "Well?"

"He's safe," I told her. "For now."

I hadn't told Gilly about the vision before calling Ezra, but she'd overheard me relay the gist of it to him. "A homemade bomb? Cripes, this dude is a maniac."

I glanced at Brady. "I don't suppose you saw the person who made the order?"

"I don't know anything about anything." He shook his head, still looking shell-shocked. "Abby Salinger, my boss, took the order." He frowned. "You'll have to ask her."

I didn't know the owner of the florist. I'd ordered flowers for delivery over the years for funerals and such, but I'd never been to the shop. I'd made all my orders by phone with a credit card. "Is she still at the store?" I asked him.

"Should be," he replied, his voice shaky. "The shop closes to customers at four, but Abby sometimes stays late making floral arrangements for the next day."

The phone number for the florist was on the side of the van. I punched in the number and waited as it rang three times before going to voicemail.

"You've reached Garden Cove Floral. Our normal business hours are nine to four, Monday through Friday, and Saturdays eleven to four. We are closed on Sunday.

If you've reached us outside of business hours and would like to make an order, go to our website and schedule an order online. Otherwise, please call back during regular business hours."

I hung up, frustration bubbling inside me. "That was useless."

Gilly picked the flowers and vase up from the floor. "No answer?" she asked.

"Just store hours," I sighed.

Ari returned from the kitchen with a roll of paper towels, dabbing at the wet spots on the carpet.

"She still might be there," Brady interjected. "She ignores the main phone after hours."

I looked at the kid blandly. "That would've been good information to have a minute ago."

Gilly glanced out the door and tapped my shoulder. "Patrol car."

Officers Jeanna Treece and Levi Walters parked and exited the marked vehicle. I'd worked with them on several cases in my capacity as a consultant, so they were both aware of my ability. Another police car pulled in behind them. When the two officers got out, Jeanna gave them orders to secure the delivery van.

"Am I in trouble?" Brady asked as they approached the house. His voice was tinged with fear.

I felt bad for the kid, but the threat of danger was too high to reassure him that everything would be okay.

As they strolled up the sidewalk, Jeanna waved at me. "Hey, Ms. Black. We have to quit meeting like this."

I shook my head. "I'd love for this to be a social call."

She jerked her thumb over her shoulder at the delivery van. "Ezra says we need to tape off the van until the forensic team can get here and go over it."

"Hey, no way," Brady protested. "I still have deliveries to make."

Levi Walters, a thin, young officer with jet-black hair and dark brown eyes, grunted at the kid. "Tough. Deliveries have been delayed." He narrowed his gaze on Brady, his expression wary. "Anything you want to tell us before we search the van?"

"Nothing I can think of," Brady replied, a worried crease lining his forehead.

I wasn't sure what Ezra told the two officers, especially over the phone, but I doubted he mentioned my vision. Not over the phone. My suspicion was confirmed when Jeanna pulled out a notepad and pen and began questioning the delivery guy.

"All right, Brady. I need to ask you a few questions. First off, give me your full name and contact details."

"Bradford Newsome," he replied with a gulp. "Eight Seven Magnolia Court."

"And your phone number?"

The young man winced, then prattled off the number with the area code. "I'm not a suspect, am I? I don't even know what's going on."

Jeanna cast her gaze in my direction. I shrugged and then shook my head. Brady seemed too clueless to be the perpetrator, but he could be a good actor. And if not the person, he could be an accomplice. However, the fact that he'd delivered the order earlier than it had been scheduled seemed to clear him of any wrongdoing.

"Who placed the order for the flowers?" Jeanna asked.

"I don't know," he whined. "Like I told the lady," he gestured at me, "my boss, Abby Salinger, took the order. You'll have to ask her if you want any details."

"The shop's closed," I told Jeanna. "I got an answering machine when I called a few minutes ago."

She arched her brow at me then turned to Brady. "Do you have Ms. Salinger's cell phone number?"

He shook his head. "No, just the shop number."

She nodded as she jotted the information down. "Are you aware of anything unusual about how the order was placed? Any special instructions?"

Brady nodded. "Abby told me to make sure the lilies got here by five on the dot and that it was really important."

"But did you see the customer?"

Brady frowned and shook his head. "I don't work in the shop or take orders." He sucked his teeth. "I don't even know what this is about. All I do is deliver flowers, that's it. I don't know anything about bombs and stuff."

The officers' faces registered alarm.

"Bomb?" Jeanna stared at me. "Detective Holden said you received threats via a flower delivery and to secure the scene." She blanched. "Is there a bomb in the van?"

"I don't think so," I replied hesitantly. "It's somewhere else." The where was anyone's guess. Now that Ezra wasn't in his truck anymore, a part of me hoped they would find it under the carriage. It chilled me to the bone to think about him being in mortal danger, but at least we'd have found it before it could do real harm.

"You got one of your, uh..." Jeanna scratched her nose to indicate my aroma-mojo.

I gave a quick nod and quietly said, "Yes. And there's a deadline." I tapped an imaginary watch on my wrist. "It's set to go off at eight o'clock."

"How do you know that?" Her brow furrowed. "Isn't your uhm, thing, about seeing memories, not the future?"

"Yeah, but whoever is doing this knows that. They planned this at least a week ago." Possibly, they'd been planning this for a lot longer and were just now putting their plan into action. "They wanted the florist to deliver the flowers to me at exactly five o'clock, and in the memory, they said I had three hours."

Jeanna hissed a curse under her breath.

Levi turned to Brady, his demeanor and tone demanding. "Did anything seem off when you loaded up your delivery?"

The kid recoiled. "The only thing was the smell." He wrinkled his nose and curled his lip in disgust. "It was intense. It gave me a headache and made me sick to my stomach. That's the only reason I delivered them early."

Again, the early delivery was an indication of his

innocence in the matter. I was grateful for the extra time, though I wasn't sure how much half an hour would help. The clues, if the person who sounded like Morgan Freeman gave any, were vague. EZ Holden as EZ Reader. Was there something in the play on words? Or was the bomber merely trying to be clever?

Jeanna's lips pursed as she put her notebook away. She glanced at Brady. "Stay put, Mr. Newsome. We're not done with you yet."

"Yes, ma'am." Brady jammed his hands in his pocket as he looked down at the carpet and avoided eye contact with the officer.

Jeanna's eyes narrowed on him as she scanned his face. "You sure there's nothing else you need to tell us? You seem pretty nervous for *just* delivering flowers."

Brady rubbed the back of his neck, his face flushed. "Well..."

Levi stepped closer, his voice stern. "Spit it out, kid. We don't have all day."

Brady swallowed hard. "I might have some weed gummies in the van. They're legal now, but still..." He spread his palms wide. "I haven't taken any today. I wait until I get home."

Jeanna and Levi exchanged a glance. It didn't take a psychic to know that people, in general, don't drive around with weed in their vehicles if they are only using it at home. Even so, with the new marijuana laws in effect, I wasn't sure that was a battle the two officers wanted to take on right now. Besides, the potential bomb took precedence.

"Three-hour deadline," I reminded them.

Jeanna clucked her tongue. "Okay," she said. "Thanks for being honest, Brady. Just sit tight while we sort this out. We'll need to have a look at those gummies, too."

Brady nodded, relief and anxiety mingling on his face. "I'll cooperate. Whatever you need."

I glanced at the van, filled with Starfighter lilies, and wondered if I could get a second vision from them. With the short timetable and the imminent danger, it was worth a shot.

"Jeanna, I need to smell those lilies," I said, stepping forward. "The ones in the van, I mean."

Levi raised an eyebrow. "You think it'll help?"

I nodded. "It's worth a shot. If there are any more memory clues, the strong scent of the lilies might trigger them."

Jeanna stepped in front of me. "I can't let you approach the van. Not until we've done a sweep and cleared it of any IEDs. Detective Holden would have my badge if I put you in danger, and I like my job."

IED stood for improvised explosive devices, and there had been too much of that in the news over the past decade. Still, I never thought it was something I'd have to worry about in Garden Cove.

I acquiesced to her decision with a nod. Gilly then

piped up, "Hey, if Nora can't go to the flowers, maybe you could bring the flowers to Nora?"

More police cars arrived, along with an unmarked blue sedan. Reese McKay was in the driver's seat, and Ezra got out on the passenger side.

My heart dipped. Knowing he was safe and seeing him safe were two different beasts. I skirted around Jeanna and went outside to meet him.

"Well?" I asked expectantly.

He shook his head. "No bomb."

I gave him a quick embrace, thankful that he hadn't been in danger. "What now? We don't have much time to stop whatever this guy has planned."

"If he has anything planned," I heard someone say.

I pivoted my gaze to scan the officers and saw Broyles. Ugh.

Before the jerk could say more, Ezra pinned him with a go-ahead-punk, make-my-day stare.

"Just what I need," I muttered.

Ezra's lips thinned. "He's my explosives expert."

"Great," I said flatly. "I wish I knew why the guy hates me so much."

"He doesn't hate you," Ezra said, but not in any way that convinced me. "It doesn't matter. He's good at his job, and he'll do it."

Broyles was ex-military, but Ezra hadn't told me any details of his service record, and I hadn't asked.

"Let's go over the memory again," Ezra said. "Maybe something in it will give us a place to start."

"If you can make heads or tails out of it." It was hot outside for late May, but a shiver skittered along my skin. I crossed my arms over my chest. "He was humming the EZ Reader theme song. The one from Electric Company."

Ezra arched a brow.

Moments like these reminded me of the cultural age gap between us. Electric Company had been the edgier cousin of Sesame Street and my favorite show when I was in elementary school. It had gone off the air in 1977, a decade before Ezra had even been born.

"Morgan Freeman was EZ Reader on the show," I explained. "He had this theme song they would play at the beginning of all his skits."

"Go on," Ezra said.

"The bomber used Freeman's voice and sang, 'EZ Holden, that's his name. EZ Holden will play my game.'"

Ezra's eyes darkened. "Anything else?"

"'Time's not your friend, Nora. It's ticking away. Will you find the bomb before it finds its prey? For someone with your gifts, it should be easy.'" I rubbed my arms. "He emphasized 'easy,' which made me think he was talking about you." I met Ezra's gaze. "He finished with, 'I hope you can speed read, Hero. Tick tock. You have three hours before the clock runs out.'"

"EZ Reader," Gilly, who'd come up behind me, commented. "Maybe he was talking about places where you read, like the library or a bookstore."

"Maybe," I mused. I turned my gaze to the van. "I

think we need more information. If I can surround myself with the flowers, like the person in my vision, maybe, just maybe..." If the bomb went off before we could find it and people were injured or worse, I wasn't sure I could forgive myself. If it hadn't been for my clairolfaction, or as Gilly sometimes called it, my scratch-n-sniff psychic ability, this wouldn't be happening.

Ezra placed a comforting hand on my shoulder. "Whatever happens, Nora, this isn't your fault. Remember that. You're not responsible for the behavior of a psychopath."

"I know that logically," I said quietly. "It doesn't make me feel less responsible, though."

"Easy's right," Gilly added. "Bad people do bad things. If this guy wasn't targeting your ability, he'd be targeting something else." She put her arm around my waist. "He's made a huge mistake, though. Big!" she said, mimicking a line from Pretty Woman.

"Oh, yeah? And what's that?" I asked her.

"He picked the wrong girl to mess with." She kissed my cheek. "You'll catch him, Nora. You always do."

I hoped she was right, but for the first time, I had doubts. It was easier to catch criminals when they were unaware of my ability. Finding one who was using it against me was a whole different game.

"Van's clear," Broyles shouted. "No IEDs or explosives of any kind."

"You sure?" Ezra asked.

Broyles held up a handheld device that looked like a radiation detector, and added, "I ran the sniffer over every inch and wiped it down with some trace paper. No explosive residue anywhere. If there was anything in or around this vehicle, I would've found it."

Ezra waved his acknowledgment.

"Sniffer?" I asked him. "What's that?"

"It's a portable explosive trace detector," he explained. "It detects explosives and explosive residue, and the trace paper will color when it comes in contact with any residue."

"Like at airport security when they run those paper disks over your luggage."

"Just the same." He nodded. "Van's clear. You want to try again for another vision?"

I stared at the van for a moment, then nodded. "I think I have to." Now wasn't the time for caution. Lives were at stake. "We're running out of time."

SEVEN

Ezra put Reese in charge of tracking down Abby Salinger. After, he cleared the area around the van of police officers. Brady hadn't been exaggerating the intensity of the scent. This many Starflight lilies together in an enclosed space was pungently over-whelming.

"You okay?" Ezra asked.

"As okay as I can be," I replied, sitting on the floor amongst the bouquets.

"Take your time."

I quirked a smile. "But not too much."

"Exactly," he said.

I closed my eyes and inhaled deeply.

I'm back in the white room amongst the flowers. The figure in white takes a phone from his hoodie's pocket and runs a finger over the screen. In Morgan Freeman's voice, he says a word that was more at home in Samuel Jackson's mouth. He shoves his hand under his shirt, and I can't see what he's up to until the glove lands on his lap.

My pulse jumps as I realize he can't open the phone screen with the glove on. I see a bit of skin on the back of a hand before he gets it tucked all the way under the hoodie again. Our culprit is white. That's information I didn't have before.

In the voice of Sir Ian McKellen as Gandalf the Gray, he says, "Gather quickly where secrets are told, and past sins run hot and cold. Where friends gather, strong but few, find the bomb before it strikes true. Twelve rules to rule them all. Seek them out before they fall. Tolkiens of victory in their palm won't protect them against my bomb."

The white-masked creep starts laughing, and I hate that I'll never see "Lord of the Rings" in the same way again.

When I came out of the memory, my stomach roiled as the taco I'd eaten earlier threatened to reappear in my lap. I scrambled from the van, gulping for fresh air.

Ezra had his hand on my back as I retched and dry heaved.

"How bad is it?" he asked when the heaving stopped.

My throat was sore and scratchy as I rasped. "I think Gilly might be right. Is there anyone at the library tonight?"

He snapped his fingers, and Officer Treece jogged over. "Call the library," he said to her. "See if they have any events on tonight."

"On it," she replied. She took out her phone and did a quick Google search. "Yep," she confirmed. "They are having a Goosebumps Family Night." She held up the screen to show the details. "It starts at six."

He nodded at Jeanna. "Call the librarian and tell them to cancel the event and evacuate the building." Ezra's gaze turned to me as the officer stepped away to make her call. "What did you see this time?" he asked.

I took a deep breath, still tasting the acrid memory of bile in my mouth. "It's... it was all so strange."

Ezra's eyes stayed locked on mine. His expression was encouraging but also patient. I appreciated that he didn't waste time with unnecessary questions.

"I was in the white room again, the one filled with flowers. The figure in white, our suspect, pulled out a phone. He had to remove his glove to use it, and I saw his skin. He's white. I didn't know that before." I paused, watching Ezra's face as he absorbed this new piece of information.

"He started speaking, but it wasn't his voice. It was like he was channeling different voices, famous ones. First, he sounded like Morgan Freeman, then Gandalf from 'Lord of the Rings.' I'm sure that's why he had to access his phone. Ari brought up earlier that he's probably using a voice-changing app. They have them for celebrity voices."

"That makes a lot of sense," Ezra said. "More than impersonators."

I nodded my agreement. "It was unsettling. He put on Ian McKellen's voice and recited a strange poem."

His brow furrowed. "Can you remember it?"

I tried to recall the words exactly. "He said, 'Gather quickly where secrets are told, and past sins run hot and cold. Where friends gather, strong and few, find the bomb before it strikes true. Twelve rules to rule them all. Seek them out before they fall. Tolkiens of victory in their palm won't protect them against my bomb.'"

Ezra's eyes widened slightly. "It sounds like he's referencing 'Lord of the Rings.' I can see why you thought of the library."

"That was Gilly's thought earlier, with the EZ Reader taunt. So, when he started talking about Tolkien, it felt like she might have the right of it."

"Seems likely," he agreed. "But weird."

"Right?" I shivered, and Ezra rubbed his hands along the sides of my arms. "It's a guess."

"At this point, we have to follow the clues where they lead," he said. "Anything else?"

"He started laughing. The kind of laugh that makes your skin crawl."

Ezra's hand tightened on my arm. "The library is having an event tonight. It could be considered a gathering of friends."

"But it's Goosebumps, not The Hobbit," I said.

"Maybe the voice changer didn't have a setting for Jack Black." He gave me a half-smile before his expression went grim. "Anything else you remember?"

I closed my eyes, trying to pull any last detail from the vision. "No, just the sense of urgency. We need to find this clown, Ezra. And fast."

He nodded, his jaw set in determination. "We'll find him. We have to."

"I just hope we're not too late." I felt the immense weight of the countdown. Three hours was a long time for a root canal, but with the stakes this high, the time would breeze by quickly.

Ezra waved Broyles over. "Take a team to the library, make sure the building has been evacuated, then do a quick grid search and watch for traps."

Broyles looked doubtful. "Are we even sure there's an explosive device? Where's the evidence?"

Ezra scowled. "You're an asset to our department, Broyles, but that doesn't mean I won't bench you. You don't have to trust Ms. Black's ability, but the chief and I trust her. If that's not good enough for you to follow orders, then maybe special operations isn't the right team for you."

"Broyles, quit being a jackass," Reese McKay chided as she charged over to us. "You know how to follow orders, right?"

The man bristled with irritation. "I know how to follow orders."

"Good." Ezra lifted his chin to the man as if daring him to take a punch. "Then get to it. Call me immediately if you find anything."

I didn't want to defend the obnoxious man, but he was right about the fact that there wasn't any real evidence of a bomb. "Look," I said. "I can only go by what I see in my visions. Most of the time, the memories are genuine moments in someone's life, but this person, whoever they are, has found a way to attach emotional memories to scents in a manufactured scenario. Was he holding a bomb in his hand with a timer attached? I don't know. That's what it looked like, though. And I think the bullets in the popcorn kettle were dangerous enough to take this monster seriously." I pointed to the van. "Those flowers were sent to me with a card that claimed to be from EZ. This person wanted me to think it was Ezra so I'd take a big whiff. Even if you don't believe I have the ability to see what I see, you have to believe someone is pulling the strings on this game of psychic chicken."

Broyles squinted at me. "Maybe it's you. Maybe you're the game master."

"That's enough," Ezra barked.

Reese put her hand on Broyles' chest and pushed him backward. "Go," she ordered, like a good second in command. "Go do your job unless this is your way of putting in your notice."

He scoffed. "I'll report back when I have the library squared away." He dipped his head with grudging respect at Reese before rotating on his heel and marching over to a gathered group of four officers. After a short conversation, they got in their vehicles and drove off like a caravan of travelers.

"He's a dick," I said once they were gone.

"Understatement," Ezra replied.

Reese, who wore plain clothes like Ezra, adjusted her

stance. She had a hip holster on, and she looked badass. "He's all right." She tugged at the end of a strand of her copper-red hair. "He's got a bit of a chip on his shoulder from blindly following orders in the military, even when it went against his own moral compass."

"You've gotten to know him pretty well," Ezra commented.

Her cheeks reddened. "I've been on a couple of cases with him. We talked. He's a good cop."

Ezra's expression remained bland. "Maybe you should go oversee his progress at the library since you work so well with him. Make sure the place is completely evacuated. Better to be safe."

Reese gave him a two-finger salute. "You got it, boss." She frowned, then said, "We were able to contact Abby Salinger. She's still at her shop. She said she would be there for another hour. I'll text you the address if you want to go interview her." She winked at me. "Maybe take a consultant along."

Ezra shook his head, a slight grin on his lips as she walked off.

"You want to take a field trip to Garden Cove Floral?"

"I do," I told him.

Ezra's smile was so genuine as he gazed down at me with his lovely green eyes. He caressed my cheek. "That's my girl." He glanced at Gilly, who was waiting on the porch for me. "You better let your girl know what's up, and then we'll get going."

"What about the van?" Brady was sitting on one of

my porch chairs, his head down, and elbows on his knees. "The kid is worried about losing his job."

"Once we get the Starfighter lilies out, he's free to finish his deliveries."

"You old softie," I said with great affection. I linked my arm in his. "Give me a minute to talk to Gilly, and I'll meet you at the..." I frowned. "Reese was your ride."

Ezra chuckled. "I guess you're my ride now."

"Is that a euphemism?"

He laughed again. "Only if you want it to be."

I gave him a friendly elbow to the ribs as we walked toward the house. I was eager to talk with Abby Salinger at her store. Maybe there would be a scent at the shop that would lead me to a genuine memory. It was a long shot, but with little else to go on, I had to take it. I could be wrong about the library. I could be wrong about the bomb. The staged memories could be complete tricks meant to send me and the police on a wild goose chase. Even so, I had to keep trying until we found the explosive device or the deadline ran out. I wouldn't forgive myself if I didn't.

EIGHT

G arden Cove Floral was in the same shopping center as the local grocery store. The warm air outside carried the scent of nearby restaurants on a gentle breeze. Abby Salinger met us at the front door, smiling politely but guardedly, as she let us in.

The store was filled with vibrant plants and intricate floral arrangements. Two refrigerators hummed quietly, showcasing various bouquets. The fresh aroma of stems, leaves, and clippings was invigorating. I was instantly hit with a few memory visions, but none related to the bomber.

Abby appeared to be in her mid-thirties. She was tall and thin with dark brown hair, pulled up into a neat bun. She wore jeans, a white top, and a floral apron that added a touch of charm to her practical outfit.

"What in the world did Brady do now?" she inquired, raising an eyebrow. "This isn't about his pot, is it? I told him if he brought that crap to work one more time, he was fired."

"This isn't about Brady," Ezra said firmly, displaying his badge. "We need to know about an order you took that was sent to Nora Black. Eight bouquets of Starfighter lilies."

"Oh, those." Abby's hand moved to her neck, her fingers brushing her skin as if to ward off the nervous energy radiating from her. "That was a special order."

Ezra crossed his arms over his chest, his expression gruff and unyielding. "Just how special was this order?"

"What's the big deal?" Abby asked, her voice tinged with confusion. "Was Ms. Black upset about the lilies?"

"I'm Ms. Black," I interjected, stepping forward. "And yeah, they upset me a lot."

Ezra stepped closer, his tone demanding, "Who ordered the flowers?"

"It wasn't like that," Abby replied defensively, her eyes darting between us. "The customer didn't really order the flowers as much as they ordered the delivery of the flowers."

"What's that supposed to mean?" I asked, narrowing my eyes.

"I mean the flowers weren't my stock. I didn't make the arrangements," Abby explained, her voice rising slightly. "If something was wrong with them, it's on the customer, not me."

"And who was this customer?" Ezra reiterated, his patience thinning. "I need a name."

"I didn't exactly get a name," Abby admitted, her shoulders slumping. "They made the order by phone."

"Did they use a credit card?" I pressed. I always used a credit card whenever I called in orders, so it made sense that she would have to have a name.

Abby shook her head, her bun wobbling slightly. "The instructions were to drop off the flowers at five o'clock on the dot. I assumed that's when you got off work or something, Ms. Black, and the customer paid in cash via an envelope left with the buckets of flowers in my alley this afternoon."

The buckets. That must have been what he was doing in the memory—putting all the flowers together for the delivery, ensuring his emotions were tied to the flowers and not some random stranger's that would spoil his plans for me.

"How much did he pay you?" Ezra asked, his tone steady but insistent.

Abby momentarily chewed on her lower lip. I suspected she was pondering how honest she should be. Finally, she admitted, "One thousand dollars."

"Holy cow," I hissed. "That's a lot of money for a flower delivery."

"I thought the same thing," she confessed, her shoulders slumping. "But the economy is tough right now. I can't turn down that kind of easy money."

Ezra gave her a sympathetic nod. "I get that, Ms. Salinger."

"Miss," she corrected, her voice suddenly light and flirty. "I'm not married."

"Good to know," Ezra replied professionally. He glanced at me, and I rolled my eyes. Turning his attention back to Abby, he said, "I'm afraid I'm going to need the envelope and the cash if you still have it."

"The cash is going to be a problem," she said, her face tightening. "I used it to pay off one of my debts."

Ezra looked unhappy. "I'm going to need the name of the debtor."

Her expression soured. "Bellmore Parker."

"The guy who owns Parker's Landing and Lakeshore Resort?" Ezra asked, incredulous.

"He also owns this shop." She gestured around the store, her eyes narrowing. "I was behind on rent, and he'd been dogging me hard for it."

Ezra shook his head, a frown deepening his features. "How much do you owe him?"

She harrumphed, crossing her arms. "More than a thousand, but at least it got him off my butt for a few days."

"We need to go check out the back where he dropped off the flowers," Ezra told her.

"Be my guest." She gestured to the back of the store. "The door is just past my office."

"After you," Ezra said.

She huffed her annoyance but complied.

Ezra and I followed her past the front counter and down a short hall to a large metal door with a lighted exit sign above the frame. The passage in the alley was wider than I had imagined, not like the narrow space we had behind Scents and Scentsability. Abby's alley was spacious enough for a delivery vehicle to park and unload. The ground was marked with various tire tracks and a few potholes. A faint smell of damp earth and rotting vegetation lingered in the air, mixing with the hum of an industrial-sized air conditioner.

"Let's start where the flowers were left," Ezra suggested.

Abby pointed to a spot near the shop's back door. "Just over there. Eight buckets, and the flowers were already trimmed, wrapped, and in vases."

We walked over to the area, and I knelt down, running my fingers lightly over the ground. The concrete was cold and rough, but there were faint scuff marks and a few crushed petals. My heart raced as I tried to focus, hoping to trigger another vision.

"Anything?" Ezra asked, watching me closely.

I shook my head, frustrated. "Nothing. It's like trying to catch smoke with my bare hands."

Ezra nodded and began to inspect the surroundings more thoroughly. He moved a few boxes aside, checking for anything unusual. I followed his lead, examining the trash bins and the corners where the shadows were deepest. A sudden chill ran down my spine, and I turned quickly, half-expecting to see someone watching us.

"What is it?" Ezra's voice was tense, his hand

instinctively reaching for the small of his back where he kept his gun.

"I don't know," I admitted, my voice barely above a whisper. "It's just a feeling."

He gave me a reassuring nod and continued his search. I noticed something glinting in the low light as I moved closer to the wall. I bent down and picked up a small, metallic object, carefully picking it up from the edges so that I wouldn't smudge the surface. It was a Susan B. Anthony dollar.

"Ezra, look at this," I said, holding it up for him to see.

He came over and took the coin from me, holding it on the edge as well, as he inspected it closely. He took a plastic bag from his pocket and dropped the dollar inside. "It might be nothing, but it won't hurt to get fingerprints."

Ezra looked around the alley, his jaw flexing as he chewed his thoughts. "We need to find out who this guy is and why he's targeting you. I don't think we're going to find the answers here."

I nodded, feeling a surge of resolve. "All we can do is try. There has to be more clues here." I felt desperately responsible. "We can't give up."

Ezra shook his head. "We're not giving up."

We moved to the tire tracks next, examining them closely. Ezra crouched down, running his fingers along the indentations. "These tracks look fresh. It could be from the vehicle he used."

I looked around, noticing a security camera mounted on the corner of the building adjacent to the flower shop. "Hey, look, there's a camera," I told Ezra. "Do you think it might have caught something?"

He followed my gaze and stood up, a spark of hope in his eyes. "It's worth checking out. If the footage is recent, we might get a clear view of the vehicle and even the driver."

"That camera doesn't work," Abby said. "Someone cut the line last week, and Mr. Parker hasn't gotten anyone out here to fix it."

Well, crap. "That's a dead end."

"We know more than we did, but less than we need to," Ezra said. "What about the envelope?" he asked Abby.

"Sorry," she said. "Like the money, it's gone. I threw it away this afternoon before the trash pick-up today. It's sitting in the city landfill right now."

"Double crap," I said. I met Ezra's gaze. "Can we go to the library? Maybe there's something there. Something I can see."

"See..." Abby's face lit up. "Say, are you that lady from the paper? The one who sees the future and gets in people's heads?"

"No," I replied. "Not me. No future foresight and no head seeing." Though if I had those particular abilities, it would've made finding this guy much easier.

"No," Abby countered. "The letter said Nora Black. That's you."

"Oh, lord." I shook my head. "Ezra, time to go."

He gave me a tight smile. "Yep." He turned to Abby. "Come down to the station tomorrow and fill out a witness statement."

She flashed him with a heated look. "What am I supposed to have witnessed?"

"Just give a statement about the flowers and how the order was made," he told her. "Thank you for your cooperation."

"Why don't you give me your number?" she asked him. "If I remember anything new, I'll call you. Or maybe I'll call you just because."

Ezra shook his head. "I think we're good. If you need to talk to me, you can call the station."

It was petty, but I internally squealed with delight at her forlorn and rejected expression. As we walked back through the shop and out to the front parking lot, I gave Ezra a nudge with my shoulder.

He grinned. "You okay with how I handled that?"

"Absolutely." I gave him another nudge. "It was kind of hot."

"Kind of?" He raised his brows.

I barked a laugh. "What? You want a cookie?"

"Only if they're your cookies." Ezra's phone rang before I could respond. "Detective Holden," he said when he answered. "What you got for me?" After several grunts and uh-huhs, he finally said, "You couldn't find anything?" He paused as the person on the other side of the call spoke again. "Okay, good idea. Head over there and check it out but leave a patrol car outside the library tonight. Don't let anyone back inside. Not until tomorrow, just in case."

"No bomb at the library?" I asked when he disconnected the call.

"No bomb," he confirmed. "A lot of angry families, though."

I grimaced. "This is going to be a tough one to explain."

"It would've been tougher explaining mass casualties if there had been a bomb and we'd done nothing."

"Good point," I told him. Gah. My guilt meter rose. I'd ruined an entire event because I couldn't figure out the clues in my vision. "What do we do now? Should we see if Bellmore Parker still has the cash?" I was grasping at straws now.

"I'm not sure how that will lead us to the suspect." Parker sighed. "Why don't I take you home?"

"What about you?"

"Reese suggested a used bookstore, Good Time's Book Nook."

"I've heard of that place," I said. "It's not in town." The Book Nook was out past the resorts in a building that used to be a square dance barn. It had been a swap shop for a while and a flea market before this latest venture. "Do they have something going on tonight?"

"Apparently, they're having an auction," Ezra said.

Adrenaline sped my pulse.

"You think of something?" he asked.

"The EZ Reader clue. He said he hoped I was a speed reader. Auctioneers talk with a lot of speed..." I shook my head. "It's dumb. I'm grasping for a connection."

"It's something." He opened the car door for me. "You want to come along?"

I raised my brows at him. "You know I do." I'd go stir-crazy at home. Besides, the bomber might be methodical with the memories he had revealed to me, but he couldn't guard against all his memories. He'd make a mistake, and when he did, we would catch him.

NINE

The lake was a hub of activity. Fishing boats, houseboats, and pontoons trolled up and down the water. Families with small children, groups of teenagers, and young adults all enjoyed the warm weather and the low-hanging sun. It was almost seven now, and the sun wouldn't completely set until eight-forty-five. There was still time to enjoy the day. Portman's on the Lake was sponsoring a raft race tomorrow, a tradition for over two decades, where contestants had to build their own rafts by hand and traverse three miles from Portman's to the dam and back without their rafts falling apart. Mason, Ari, and a few of their friends had decided to enter this year.

I'd been looking forward to cheering them on, but after the letter to the paper and the guy playing games with people's lives because of me, I wasn't sure what I'd be doing.

Good Time's Book Nook was two miles past the last of the resorts on Highway 44 west of town. I'd driven past the place many times before, but I'd never seen it with so many cars out front. Auctions were a draw for rural areas, but I was betting half the people here were city tourists looking for a different kind of adventure. The Good Time's Book Nook itself looked like a large metal outbuilding, with a parking lot big enough for swap meets.

"Why haven't they evacuated the area?" Ezra asked, pulling out his phone. I assumed he was calling Reese. "I just arrived," he barked. "Why are there a hundred or more people still here?"

I shuttled us around the large but full parking lot, searching for an empty space and having no luck. I saw Reese, her arm gesticulating wildly as she spoke on the phone. Broyles was at another vehicle talking with Levi and someone else.

"You've got to be crappin' bricks," Ezra said scathingly. "I'll call him. Just get in there and see if you can find anything that looks like it might blow up." He punched the disconnect button with his index finger, then dialed another number. "Chief," he said. "Why aren't we evacuating the auction? What? The mayor? She can't..." He shook his head. "This is a bunch of nonsense. If someone gets hurt, she will have more to deal with than an election. Fine," he conceded. "I get it. I don't like it, but I get it."

I spotted the backup lights of a vehicle getting ready

to leave and pulled up close enough to claim the spot when they pulled out. Other cars were also looking for parking, and I wasn't about to let them take this one from me.

"The mayor is here," Ezra groused as he got off the phone. "She's one of the sponsors for this auction. It's a freaking charity event to raise money and awareness for the community foundation." He shook his head. "More like an event to raise awareness for her campaign."

The community foundation fund was a worthwhile charity. They donated money for various programs in Garden Cove, including grants for schools, beautification projects around town, and low-interest loans for small businesses. Still, I understood and mirrored Ezra's frustration.

"The best we can do is cordon off the building and keep everyone outside until we finish our search."

"It's something," I told him. I honked at a car that tried to skirt past me for my spot as the other vehicle, a compact pickup, finally pulled out. The guy honked back and flipped me off before moving on.

I whipped into the spot before anyone else got any ideas about trying to take it from me. We were running out of time. If we didn't find the bomb by eight, it would go off. As I parked, a gnawing worry tugged at me. The Book Nook didn't feel quite right to all the clues. What if we were going down the wrong trail? With less than an hour until the deadline, I wasn't sure we had any choices left.

"I'm worried that this isn't right," I told him. "Auctioneers talk fast, and yes, this place has books, but it doesn't fit the rest."

Reese knocked on the window, and I jumped. She opened the back door and crawled inside. "What are we doing?" she asked. "What did the chief say?"

"He said the same thing. Mayor says no to shutting down and evacuating the auction."

"Broyles and his team are going over the building, but there is a lot of stuff in there left over from when it was a swap shop. A lot of things that look like can bombs. It's hard to tell what's what. A lot of false alarms so far."

"Let's go over the poem from Nora's vision again," Ezra suggested. "Break it down, line by line. Maybe we jumped too fast to the wrong conclusion."

I took a breath and tried to recite it as exactly as I could remember. "Gather quickly where secrets are told...."

Reese leaned forward from the backseat. "Secrets aren't told here."

Ezra shrugged. "Unless were talking about secrets kept in books from the characters."

"Maybe." I nodded. "And past sins running hot and cold?"

"Historical books?" he suggested.

"Friends gathering, strong and few," I continued.

"Friends might be gathering here, but this is way more than a few people."

"Maybe the guy didn't know there would be a big thing going on tonight when he planned this." Ezra scratched his chin with his thumb. "How long has this auction been on the books?"

"A few months," Reese answered. "She got the permits approved back in February."

Broyles got into the backseat on the other side. "The building is clear," he said. "We've gone over it with the sniffer and got nada." His tone sounded unsurprised. "This has been, no offense to the consultant, but a colossal waste of time."

"It's not a waste of time as long as the threat is out there," Ezra said.

"If," Broyles countered. "If the threat is out there."

Ezra heaved a noisy sigh, and I could feel his exasperation. "You can help, or you can get the hell out."

The ex-military thorn in Ezra's side responded by easing back into the seat and keeping his mouth shut. Small victories, I thought.

Ezra put his hand on my arm. "What's the next line?"

"Twelve rules to rule them all," I told him.

"The numbers wrong, if it's a Tolkien reference," Reese said. "There are twenty rings in the 'Lord of the Rings.'"

"One rules them all," Broyles contributed with a grunt.

"What else?" Ezra asked.

I continued, "The last part is to seek them out before

they fall, their Tolkiens of victory in their palms won't protect them against the bomb."

"Tolkiens?" Broyles mused. "As in more than one?"

"I'm sure that's what he said," I confirmed.

"Maybe he meant more than one book. Like several of Tolkien's novels," Reese interjected. "There's The Hobbit, and..."

"The Lord of the Rings trilogy. Other than that, just some short stories," Broyles said.

I turned to look at him.

He tucked his chin. "What? I can't know something about classic literature? Are you sure he said Tolkiens?" he asked, then added on an embarrassed mutter, "I mean, if what you're saying happened, actually happened."

"I am pretty sure," I answered him, choosing to ignore his nay-saying. "Why? What are you thinking?"

"Tolkiens in a palm. What if it's tokens. Like a coin."

"We found a Susan B. Anthony silver dollar outside the florist shop," Ezra said. "Maybe that has some significance."

"Or," Broyles countered, "The token is a chip."

My eyes widened. "Like a sobriety chip?"

He shrugged. "Twelve rules to rule them all? Could be referring to twelve steps."

"There's a meeting tonight at the Cove Community Church," I said rapidly. It started at seven-thirty." I grabbed Ezra's hand. "Tippy is celebrating her third year tonight. Pippa and Jordy were going as her family support. They're taking the babies."

"The CCC used to be the old library," Reese said. "The town sold the building to the church after they built the new library about ten years ago."

I'd already started the car and was backing out before Ezra could say, "Son of a—"

BY THE TIME we got on the highway, heading back to town, I had three police cars for an escort. One was in front of me and two behind me, lights flashing and sirens blaring as we sped towards Cove Community Church.

Reese called the threat in, dispatching nearby officers to the building to evacuate anyone inside. Despite these efforts, I couldn't shake the fear for my friends' safety. Ezra had repeatedly tried to contact Jordy and Pippa, but their phones went straight to voicemail.

I gripped the steering wheel, knuckles white with tension, restraining myself from flooring the gas pedal and overtaking the police escort, which seemed agonizingly slow.

The dash clock read seven forty-eight. "We're not going to make it," I muttered, tapping my fingers anxiously on the wheel.

"We'll make it," Ezra assured me, his tone firm. He

leaned forward, eyes fixed on the road. "Reese, any confirmation that anyone has arrived on scene?"

"Not yet," she replied, shaking her head as she checked her phone. "Most of our officers were at the auction, and those in town were dealing with a drunken disorderly at the Rose Palace Resort. Everyone's at least five minutes away. They won't get there much before we do."

That wasn't what I wanted to hear. "Try Pippa again," I urged, my voice tight. I racked my brain for anyone else who might be at the AA meeting but came up blank. "Do you all know anyone who might be at the meeting?" It was a long shot, but I had to ask. Reese's cousin Fiona, a young woman who'd been murdered a few years ago, had been in Narcotics Anonymous. When none of them answered in the affirmative, I asked, "Does the church have a contact number for the person who organizes the meetings? We need to get them out of there." The more I thought about the message, the more the AA meeting made sense. Few gather, sins of the past, twelve steps, a token... Why hadn't I figured it out sooner? Maybe because "EZ Reader" didn't seem to fit an Alcoholics Anonymous meeting. Even the fact that the church used to be a library didn't tick all the boxes.

I hoped we were wrong. I hoped we weren't too late.

"Still no answer," Ezra said, frustration evident in his clenched jaw. "They probably silenced their phones for the meeting."

"Pippa's been so excited about tonight. Tippy has

really come a long way since arriving in Garden Cove. She even baked the cake for Tippy's celebration." A chilling thought struck me, and I stiffened. "What if he chose the meeting because he knew Tippy would be there? Is he targeting the people I care about?"

EZ Holden, that's his name. EZ Holden will play my game.

The psycho playing the terrible game had mentioned Ezra specifically. "Time's not your friend, Nora. That's what he said in the first vision when he was taping the timer to the bomb," I recalled, voice trembling. "Will you find the bomb before it finds its prey? What if he meant 'pray,' as in the serenity prayer? Don't they say it at the end of every meeting?"

Broyles made a noise of frustration from the back-seat, shifting restlessly. I heard him speaking into his phone, "Hey. Yeah, I'm okay. Are you at the meeting at Cove Community Church tonight?"

I glanced at Ezra. His eyes narrowed, his scowl deepening.

"I need you to announce that everyone needs to evacuate the building," he instructed the person on the other end, his tone commanding. "Now. There's a bomb threat. The police are on their way." I looked in the rearview mirror and saw Broyles nodding. "Thanks. See you in a few."

"Who was that?" Reese asked, her brow furrowed.

Broyles frowned, his shoulders slumping slightly. "My sponsor."

"I didn't know you were in AA," Reese said, her voice tinged with anger and hurt.

"It's anonymous for a reason," Broyles replied, his tone softening as he looked down.

"You should've called sooner," I scolded him, glaring over my shoulder. "Lives are in danger."

"Are they, though?" he replied doubtfully, crossing his arms. "I'm still not sure I believe you."

"And yet," Ezra pointed out, raising an eyebrow, "you called your sponsor."

Broyles didn't respond, staring out the window. Had his drinking been the reason he left the military? Was that why he'd come to Garden Cove for a fresh start?

I glanced at Ezra to see if he knew about Broyles' past with alcohol. He shook his head slightly. The phone call, revealing himself as a recovering alcoholic, had cost Broyles personally.

"Thank you," I told him, my voice softening. "Thank you for making the call." It was seven fifty-four now. I could only hope the call hadn't been made too late.

TEN

B y the time we arrived at the church, it was eight-oh-one, according to my car clock. The sun was starting to set, and the old stone church stood eerily against the red sky. Two police cars and an ambulance. Less than twenty civilians were standing around the parking lot, their faces masks of confusion and concern.

"See," Broyles said smugly, crossing his arms over his chest. "It's past your deadline, and no bomb. All you've done is invade a lot of privacy."

The people who attended AA meetings on birthdays knew that families participated in those nights. Anyone wishing to remain anonymous would have avoided the event. However, I didn't bring this up because Broyles was right about one thing—there hadn't been a bomb. Had I gotten it wrong again? Had the explosion happened somewhere else and I, worried about my friend, jumped on this lead because it would be too costly to be wrong? Maybe.

As I parked, I scanned the crowd for Pippa and her family, squinting against the flashing lights.

"I see them," Ezra said, pointing to the right side of the parking lot. "There."

I noisily let out the breath I'd been holding. When the engine was off, I opened the door and scrambled from the car. "Pippa!" I shouted, waving my arms to get her attention.

A thunderous boom emanated from the building, making the ground tremble. Instinctively, I covered my head and dropped to the ground, my heart pounding. But there was no rain of debris.

"Everyone, get away from the building!" Broyles shouted. A part of me felt vindicated as he stared at me, his eyes wide with disbelief. "No one comes within fifty feet of the place until we know there's not a secondary device." When the crowd seemed frozen in place, he bellowed, "Move, people! This is not a drill."

"We're going to have to call the DHS," Reese said, her voice calm despite the chaos. "They'll want to investigate."

"This isn't a terrorist," I said, feeling light-headed with shock.

"Someone put a bomb inside a church full of people," Reese disagreed. "Regardless of the reason, it's terrorism."

I nodded as I searched for Pippa again. She, Jordy,

Tippi, and the babies were across the lot, watching the horror unfold with wide eyes.

The front door of the building was open, and a thick cloud of white smoke billowed out into the lot, spreading like an ominous fog.

"That's smoke," I said, not caring if I sounded like Captain Obvious.

"No one goes inside," Ezra ordered, stepping forward authoritatively. "Not until the fire department arrives."

"What if someone is still inside?" Reese asked, glancing nervously at the smoke.

Broyles spoke up, "Detective Holden's right. We don't have respirators or fireproof clothes. It sucks, but we have to wait."

"Oh, my God!" someone exclaimed, retching. "What's that smell?"

Within seconds, people who had been frozen in place were now scrambling toward us, covering their faces. A few had yanked their shirts over their noses, their eyes wide with fear.

"What's going on?" I asked, but before anyone could answer, a pungent odor of rotten eggs, magnified a thousand times, filled the parking lot, clinging to the humidity in the air. I gagged as the stench filled my nostrils, and the taste hit the back of my throat.

"It's toxic gas!" someone screamed. "We're being gassed!" Panic ensued as people started screaming and running in all directions.

My eyes were watering so hard that I couldn't see

who took my arm. Whoever it was, I let them lead me away from the awful stench, stumbling over the uneven ground.

"Down, down," a man shouted. He was wearing tan camouflage gear and jumped behind a rusty white truck. His top had the name BROYLES over his pocket.

There was an explosion and then another. The screams that followed chilled me to the bone, echoing in the night.

"Gas, gas, gas!" someone else hollered, their voice panicked.

"Dave's down," Broyles shouted, his voice breaking. "We can't leave him there."

"Broyles," another man said urgently. "Get your mask on!"

I saw a tall man, also in fatigues, throwing a gas mask over his blurred face as he ran into the street, dragging another man who had burns all over his arms.

"Come on, Dave, man," the tall man said as he pulled the wounded soldier across the road. "You're going to be fine. Just hang in there."

Broyles dragged him around the truck. He took a knife out and started cutting off Dave's shirt and pants, his hands steady despite the chaos.

"This doesn't usually happen until the second date," Dave wheezed, his voice weak but trying to be humorous.

"Shut up, idiot," Broyles said with a chuckle, though his eyes were filled with worry. "You're covered in sulfur mustard. Have to get this shit off you before it does more damage."

"God, it stinks," Dave coughed, his face contorted with pain. "It's like someone crapped their pants all over me and in my lungs." He moaned, the sound raw with agony. "Only, the crap is scalding toxic gas eating my skin off."

"I need some help over here! Medic!" Broyles shouted, his voice strained. He scraped dirt and dust from the ground, rubbing it all over Dave's exposed skin and brushing it away. "Hang on, Dave. Help's coming."

As I emerged from the vision, Broyles practically carried me to the other side of the road. "Something's wrong," he shouted. "We need a medic over here." His arm was around my back, supporting my weight. "Did you get any gas on you?" he asked, staring into my eyes with horror. He looked like he'd seen a ghost. "Are you in pain?"

"I'm okay," I assured him as I regained my balance. "I'm not in any pain." I looked around. "Where's Ezra?"

Broyles pointed. "He's over there."

Ezra was with a paramedic, helping a woman who had been injured in the rush to escape the church. I worried he was too close to the caustic fumes.

"Do you think it's sulfur mustard?" I asked Broyles.

His eyes widened. "Why would you think that?"

"I..." Should I tell him what I'd seen in my vision? The man was already skittish around me. Would revealing this confirm that personal privacy wasn't safe around me? I decided to test the waters. "I had a vision when the odor hit."

"About the bomber?" His voice was wary.

I shook my head. "About you. It was your memory."

"Bullshit."

"You were in combat."

"Lady," he ground out sarcastically, "I've been in a lot of combat. You don't need a crystal ball to guess that."

"There were two explosions, and someone yelled gas, gas, gas. Your friend Dave was in the street. He was burning, you—"

"Enough," he said, but the steam had left his tone.

"There was the scent of rotten eggs," I continued. "You said it was sulfur mustard."

"You saw that?" He looked around as if trying to find an escape route. "From the scent?"

"It must've triggered your emotional connection to the memory," I told him. "I wasn't trying to see it, and I won't ever talk about it again."

"Piss poor time to be sober," he muttered.

"Your friend Dave, did he..."

Broyles shook his head. "It got in his lungs. He didn't make it."

"I'm truly sorry."

"It was a long time ago." He waved off my sympathy. The motion was jerky and final, but I wasn't fooled.

I guessed it hadn't been long enough if the pain in his expression was any indication. His grief had been freshly renewed thanks to the church bomb.

"Okay," I said, resisting the urge to put a comforting hand on his arm. His rigid body language told me it would be unwelcome. "I'm okay. You can go and help. I'll be fine now."

He gave me a curt nod and returned to the parking lot to join the other first responders.

I found Pippa and her family waiting at the corner and made a beeline for them.

Pippa hugged me immediately. "What in the world is happening?" She had tears in her eyes. "Did someone call in the bomb threat?"

"In a way," I said. How could I explain the last three hours in any way that made sense right now? It was too much, and she would have more questions than I wanted to answer. "I'll tell you all about it, but later, okay? I'm just glad you guys are safe."

"I'm scared as all get out, but you're right. We're safe, and that's all that matters. But damn it, all I want to do right now is go home, lock the doors, and never leave my house again."

"I have the same impulse," I said. "If only hiding from the world paid well, I'd make it my full-time job."

She rewarded me with an amused smile. "Same."

"Can anyone tell me what's happening?" a man asked. I turned to see Edgar Jones, his arm in a sling. Poor guy couldn't catch a break today.

"I thought you'd still be in the hospital. What are you doing here?"

His face colored. "The surgery was outpatient. They let me go home after the anesthesia wore off. As to why

I'm here..." He inclined his head to the building. "It was a hell of a day."

Ah. Edgar was a recovering alcoholic too.

I was sympathetic. I didn't drink except socially, but I could see someone on a day like today going to the bottle. "Sorry."

"For what?" he chuckled, winced, then touched his injured shoulder. "I've been saved twice today. I must have an angel on my shoulder."

"Sounds about right."

Tippi threw her arms around me from behind. "I didn't even get to eat my cake, Nora."

I patted her hands. "I'm sure Pippa will make you another one."

"The hell I will," Pippa teased. "Nora can make the next one."

"Only if you want it to taste like cardboard." I laughed. "Kidding. I'll buy you one from the bakery, and it will taste divine."

JP was crying in his dad's arms. Jordy bounced the infant as he rotated his upper body back and forth. Jordy's long hair was tied up in a makeshift man bun. He had tattoos down both arms and his neck. He looked rough and tumble but was the sweetest and most patient man I'd ever met.

Pippa held out her hands. "Come to momma," she said. Next to Jordy was a double stroller. JJ, my sweetest little goddaughter, was snoozing away inside it. The explosion had left her unfazed.

Jordy smiled. "She'll sleep through anything." He gave his son a loving look. "Unlike her brother. If these two were characters in The Princess and the Pea, JP would be the princess."

"Truth," Pippa said as she put a bottle in her son's mouth. "He is allergic to mom getting any rest." She cooed at her baby. "Isn't that right, my little sweetie Pete?"

"I can't believe there was a bomb," Tippi said. "It doesn't seem real."

I shook my head. "It sure doesn't." Even though I'd had the visions, part of me had doubted how real the man's threats were. After all, he hadn't shot up the street fair. Instead, he'd put bullets in a kettle and let the chips fall where they may. That didn't seem like the act of someone trying to hurt people. Although, he also didn't seem like a guy who cared if anyone got hurt.

I scanned the gathered group of AA attendees as the police dismissed them across the road. Weirdly, I recognized someone else in the group. It was Loretta from the shop this morning—the woman with the yellow jacket, the one who was sleeping with her friend Jackie's boyfriend.

I nudged Pippa and gestured with my chin in the woman's direction. "Recognize her?"

Pippa peered at Loretta for a moment, then her eyes brightened. "The cheater," she hissed.

I nodded. "The cheater."

Tippi leaned in. "Who are we talking about?"

I didn't answer, because Ezra walked over. He took my hand and led me away from the group. "I can't leave the scene until after the FBI gets here." He shook his head. "That smell isn't going away anytime soon."

I made a face. "It's really disgusting."

"The bureau is flying in a hazardous material specialist to test the gas fumes and a bomb specialist to investigate the IED. Broyles doesn't think it's a deadly gas. No one who has come in contact with it has any burns, and they aren't having any trouble breathing, but I don't want to take any chances."

I leaned into him. "I hope everyone got out of the building."

"Me too." He pressed his forehead to mine. "Why don't you go home? Or better yet, go home with Pippa and Jordy. I'd feel better knowing you weren't alone."

"I won't be alone. I'll have Gilly come over, or I'll go over to her place." I rubbed the back of his hand with my thumb. "Are you coming over tonight?"

He shook his head. "Mason's staying at my cabin. I kind of want to check on him. Even though there wasn't a real shooter this morning, the whole thing freaked him out."

"Freaked me out too. I'm glad you'll be with him."

"Don't worry, I'm not going to leave you alone, though. Officer Treece and Walters are going to be camped outside your place all night."

"Do you think that's necessary?"

He took me in his arms. "I absolutely do. I'll feel better knowing my people are watching out for you."

I grinned. "I'll be thinking of you."

"I'll be thinking of you."

He gave me a sweet kiss that melted the walls I'd been throwing up since the maniac started sending me memories. A hot tear blurred my vision.

"Why don't you go to my place instead?" he suggested, misinterpreting my crying. "Mason would love the extra company."

If I'd had an extra bed, I would have invited him to bring Mason over, but I didn't think it was fair to drag the kid from his own bed to sleep on my couch because I didn't want to be without him. I smiled. "I'm fine. We'll talk tomorrow."

"We'll talk tonight." He smiled back. "I'll call you when I get done here."

"It's a plan."

As I kissed Ezra goodbye, a ball of pain swelled between my ribs as I thought about my new nemesis and his plans. Was this bomb the end of it or just the beginning? He was in charge of the game right now. I was his pawn. I had to believe he'd make a mistake and soon. I just hoped it happened before he killed someone to prove whatever point he was trying to make.

ELEVEN

I t was nearly nine before I got home. Treece and Walters had followed me home and were parked on the street at the end of my driveway. I lived on a *cul de sac*, so I didn't have many neighbors to complain. I texted Ezra and Pippa to let them know I was safe and mostly sound because they'd asked me to. Afterward, I trudged to my bedroom, feeling the weight of the day's tension pulling at my shoulders.

The hot shower felt like a long-awaited embrace, and as the water poured over me, the dam I'd built around my emotions finally broke. I cried, sobs racking my body, each tear washing away the remnants of the fear I'd kept at bay while we were searching for the bomb. The reality of what could have happened—the lives that could have been lost—especially Pippa and her family—hit me like a tidal wave. The thought that someone might have targeted the AA meeting, knowing that people I loved were there, gnawed at me.

The meetings were supposed to be anonymous, but anonymity wasn't guaranteed. I'd sat in on one a few years back while investigating the death of Dolly Paris, with Gilly and Pippa in tow, and that's when we'd discovered Tippi was attending meetings. Tonight was Tippi's three-year birthday. Had my nightmare stalker used that information to punish me? The bullets placed in the popcorn stand next to my sales booth had felt like a cruel taunt. Whoever was behind this wanted to prove they were cleverer than I was, and they didn't care if they hurt the people I loved in the process.

By the time I finished my shower, I felt emotionally drained but somewhat lighter. Downstairs, the comforting aroma of lemon, fresh basil, Italian parsley, and garlic wafted up, drawing me to the kitchen. Gilly, Ari, and Gilly's husband, Scott, were waiting for me, and their presence was a balm on my frayed nerves.

Gilly had cooked lemon chicken piccata served over fettuccine with a side of pan-fried asparagus for dinner and had brought me a plate over. The whole thing was covered in fresh-grated Romano cheese. Her ex-husband Gio was a renowned chef, but in my estimation, he didn't have anything on Gilly. Her food was comforting and delicious.

"Eat up," she said, placing the dish in front of me. "I know it's one of your favorites, and I made enough to feed an army."

Scott, who looked like a perfect blend of Harrison Ford and Anderson Cooper, beamed at me. "It's the best chicken I've ever had." He put his arm around Gilly's shoulders and kissed her on the cheek. "You've outdone yourself tonight, sweetheart."

Gilly flushed with pleasure, and I smiled. Not to take away from Gilly's cooking, because, as I said before, she was excellent. But she could smear peanut butter between two slices of bread, and that man would rave about how it was the best peanut butter sandwich he'd ever had.

I took a bite, savoring the sour, bitter, and salty notes of the lemon, wine sauce, and capers. "Mmm-mmm." I hummed. "No lies detected." I gave her a grateful look. "You didn't have to do all this for me, though."

She gave me the stink-eye back. "You had coffee and a roll for breakfast, no lunch, and you barely ate any of the tacos I brought you earlier. And I know you well enough to know if I wasn't force-feeding you a meal right now, you would go to bed without eating."

I smirked. "Guilty as charged." Reaching over, I squeezed her hand. "Thank you for taking such good care of me."

"You'd do the same for me." I dug in, slicing a piece of chicken breast and wrapping it with the pasta before shoving it in my mouth. "God, this is so good," I said when I finished the bite. "You can make this for me every day."

Gilly's grin almost reached her ears. "When you finish, you'll tell us what happened tonight, right?"

I nodded as I took another bite. Gilly and Ari had been with me when the stinky flowers had arrived. Of course, they wanted to know how it all turned out. I took another bite, then another. How could I tell her that my nightmare stalker was targeting my closest loved ones? I worried for Ezra, but at least he had a gun. I would never forgive myself if something happened to Gilly, Pippa, or anyone in their families.

By the time I finished my plate, there was nowhere left to hide.

When I didn't say anything right away, Scott asked, "Should I get the murder board?"

Ari's eyes lit up. "Murder board?" She smacked her palms on the counter. "What murder board?"

I chuckled softly. When we'd stumbled over a body in a vineyard last year in June while celebrating Gilly's impending nuptials, we'd created a murder board for our investigation. It had made sense at the time since we were unfamiliar with the deceased and the suspects and had no real access to the police investigation since it was out of Ezra's jurisdiction. "No one's been murdered, so I'm not sure we need one."

"Then we'll call it a suspect board," Gilly amended.

"I wouldn't even know where to begin."

Ari took her phone from her back pocket. It was one of the new foldable phones that opened to a large screen. She slid a stylus out of the end. "Suspect board acquired," she said robotically.

Gilly giggled. "Excellent. First, what happened tonight? And before you get all, oooo, how much should I tell Gilly, I will say that Pippa called me and told me about the bomb in the church."

"Then it seems you know everything."

Ari leaned forward. "How did you figure out it was the church and not the library or bookstore?"

"I didn't do it alone. The twelve rules from the memory were the twelve steps for recovery. Tolkiens was tokens, like coins or chips." I stood up, my belly stretched full. "I must've heard him wrong in the vision."

Scott nodded. "Or he was purposefully trying to throw you off."

"Maybe." I worried that the real reason I'd heard Tolkiens is because that's what I'd expected to hear. If he left another message for me, I had to pay closer attention to the exact words. I couldn't get the stench of the bomb out of my mind. I'd never smelled anything so awful. "The church used to be the library."

"Oh, that's right," Gilly said. "I think I still have my card from there somewhere."

"Didn't you say something about Morgan Freeman in one of the visions?" Ari asked.

"Yes, he sang the EZ Reader theme song from *The Electric Company*."

"So, it's a boomer," Ari said, scribbling on her phone with the stylus.

I frowned. "What makes you think that?"

"No one born past nineteen ninety has heard of EZ Reader. Morgan Freeman as God or Morgan Freeman in the Bucket List would put our suspect at Millennial or Gen Z, but EZ Reader, total Boomer."

Scott's mouth dropped open as he looked at his wife.

Gilly shrugged. "Gen X, once again, the forgotten generation."

Scott's voice lowered as he announced, "It's ten o'clock. Do you know where your children are?"

I choked on a laugh. "Even our parents forgot about us."

Ari arched a brow at the three of us. "Old people are weird."

"Word," I said, and Gilly and I bumped knuckles before we both started laughing again.

Ari raised her hands. "Can we just agree that the suspect is probably over forty?"

I nodded. "You're probably right. The Electric Company ended in the late seventies."

"But they were still playing reruns in the early eighties," Gilly said defensively. "I would catch an episode occasionally."

Ari gave her mom an incredulous look.

"What?" Gilly shrugged. "We didn't have a gazillion channels, smartphones, computers, tablets, and so forth. We had four stinkin' channels. PBS had Sesame

Street, Zoom, and reruns of The Electric Company, and I was too old for Sesame Street." She sounded exasperated.

Scott rubbed Gilly's arm and finished with a comforting pat on the shoulder. "You've been holding that one in for a little while, haven't you, Babe?"

She snickered and shook her head. "I'm just saying."

"You're not wrong," I said in solidarity. "Reading the back of cereal boxes was how we spent our screen time."

"Not you, too, Aunt Nora." Ari grinned as she slid a hair tie over her wrist, ran her fingers through her hair, and then slid the tie over the gathered length to make a ponytail. "That doesn't change the age bracket. I stand by the assumption that he's older." She gave me a quizzical look. "Do we know it's a he?"

"No. But Ezra says it's statistically more likely to be a man."

Ari jotted down, *Age – 40+, gender – male?* "What about race?"

Good. A question I could answer with one hundred percent certainty. "I only saw his hand briefly, but his skin was light."

The corner of her mouth quirked up. "So old white dude, huh?"

"Hey," Scott said with mock offense. "I resemble that remark."

We laughed again. It felt good to be working the case with my friends, even if the crumbs led us nowhere. And they were making sure I knew that I wasn't alone. That felt even better.

Ari tapped her phone. "Give all the voices again."

"Christopher Walken, Dolly Parton, Morgan Freeman, and Ian McKellan. I think you were definitely right about the voice changer app. That's how I saw the skin on his hand. He had to remove his glove to change voices on his phone." I dabbed a pepper dot on the center island top with my index finger and flicked it away. "And this person had to have known about me and my scent ability before the letter came out in the Gazette this morning." The fact that he'd ordered the floral delivery a week earlier was definitive proof. "So it has to be someone connected to the police force or one of the cases I worked on." I didn't mention my friends because I refused to believe any of them would casually gossip about my psychic smeller.

"Okay, so let's list the arrests made with your help," Gilly said. "Let's see, there was Carl Grigsby, Lucy Jameson, which also included Big Don Portman, Phil Williams, and Burt Adler."

"You were the one who took down the self-proclaimed Garden Cove Elite?" Scott asked. "I had no idea."

That's what I meant about friends not gossiping. Gilly hadn't even told the love of her life about my past cases.

"Who else?" Ari asked.

"There was that guy Aaron from the convention," Gilly added.

I waved him off as a suspect. "I think we can assume the culprit is tied to me locally."

"Okay," she said, her voice laced with a hint of reluctance. "There's Davis Meadows. He was a real creeper." Davis had been selling stolen art on the dark web, a fact that still sent shivers down my spine. I vividly recalled the moment he'd lunged at me with a knife, the glint of malice in his eyes. Luckily, it was only a glancing blow; I'd managed to fight him off with a metal chair. The man spent a week in the hospital before he recovered enough for jail. His mother closed the art store after the arrest, but she'd stayed in town.

"Let's not overlook our esteemed ex-mayor," Scott interjected, his tone tinged with disdain.

That was the situation when Gilly and Scott first started dating, and Scott was let in on my fragrant secret, Aaron Trident. The mere mention of his name sent a chill down my spine. He had taken a life to safeguard his secrets, and when the investigation got too close, he had abducted Pippa.

The memory of that terrifying ordeal still haunted me. Pippa, brave and resourceful as always, had managed to leave me a clue using a scented lip balm she had thrown from the vehicle. She had been the first person to intentionally attach a memory to a scent for me to discover. Did the individual targeting me know she had done this? He would have had to know, wouldn't he? Additionally, Trident was the one who had leaked the story about a psychic working within the GCPD shortly after his arrest. I wouldn't discount the possibility that he had orchestrated this malevolent mess. Granted, he was in prison, but he could've solicited outside help.

I clenched my jaw as I thought about the man. "Aaron Trident definitely belongs on the list."

"That covers all the local cases," I stated, with a finality in my tone.

"Don't forget about the robbery ring," Gilly chimed in, urgency coloring her voice.

"They weren't local," I reminded her, my tone firm.

"Jane Beets of Beets' Treats was," Gilly countered. "If it weren't for you, she would have collected a significant insurance payout for her place after faking the robbery at her shop."

"But she didn't face jail time," I pointed out, feeling the need to clarify.

"But she did lose her business," Gilly insisted, conviction in her voice.

"But I don't think she was ever aware of my involvement in her case. I merely provided a tip to the police." And by police, I mean Ezra.

"Fair enough," Gilly conceded. "But that doesn't mean she didn't hear rumors."

"Fine," I nodded slowly, conceding her point. "Add Jane to the list."

"And what about the officers who know about your ability?" Ari asked. "We still need to address that group."

"I honestly can't say," I admitted with a sigh. "It could be all of the GCPD by now. It could be anyone." I hated to acknowledge it, but it was the truth. All it would take is one slip of the tongue, and anyone could find out.

I had put my phone on the charger when I got home, so it startled me when it rang. "Gah. Made me jump," I said, rising from the stool.

Gilly grabbed the phone from the counter, disconnected the cable, and handed it to me. "It's Easy," she said.

I took the phone from her and answered it. "Hey," I greeted him. "Did you make it home already?"

"Not yet," he replied. "Some EPA guys showed up with the FBI."

"That makes sense," I said. "Especially if the bomb contained toxic chemicals."

"That's the thing," Ezra said quietly. "It wasn't a chemical weapon."

"It sure smelled like one."

"No," he disagreed. "It smelled like what it was..."

"What was it?"

Gilly gestured frantically, indicating to use the speakerphone.

I rolled my eyes but said, "Hey, I'm here with Gilly, Scott, and Ari. They want me to put you on speaker."

"That's fine," he replied. "I'm not saying anything they can't hear."

I placed the phone on the center island and hit the speaker button. "Okay, you're on speaker. Tell us what you found out."

"The bomb had barely any explosives, mostly gunpowder for ignition, along with sulfur powder and sugar."

"What kind of bomb is that?" I asked.

Scott's nose wrinkled, and he made a disgusted face as he answered for Ezra. "It's a stink bomb."

"That's correct," Ezra confirmed. "The IED at the church was a homemade stink bomb with a punch. There was some metal shrapnel in the walls of the stairwell from the explosion, but it doesn't seem to have been intended to be fatal. However, if it had detonated when people were leaving the meeting, there could have been serious injuries and lung damage from inhaling the sulfur gas."

"A stink bomb," I repeated. "What is this guy playing at?" My mind went back to Shawn's description of the bullets in the popcorn kettle, and the prank was starting to sound more like what was happening. But a bomb, even a stinky one, was an escalation. Who or what would he target next? "Thanks for the update," I told Ezra. "Call me when you get home, and please, be careful."

"I don't like not being with you tonight." There was a pause, and then he said, "Or any night, for that matter. I could come over."

I appreciated the offer but knew someone else needed him more tonight. "No, go be with Mason. You have officers outside the house, and..."

"Besides," Ari interjected. "I'm staying the night with Aunt Nora. She won't be alone."

I heard his soft chuckle, and it eased the knot in my chest. "Good. Talk soon." With that, he ended the call.

"A freaking stink bomb," Gilly hissed. "What the heck?"

"Those are pretty gross," Scott added. "I made one back in college to prank a friend, and the smell didn't dissipate for months, even with a thorough cleaning and all the air freshener from the dollar store."

"It's all fun and games until someone gets skunked," Gilly teased.

I forced a smile. "This guy isn't pulling pranks for laughs. He's trying to prove some kind of point." I couldn't shake the feeling that this was just the beginning of a much darker game, and I could only hope his next stunt didn't result in someone getting killed.

TWELVE

The next morning, I rose with the sun, a rare occurrence for me as I was not a morning person. My body felt stiff and my brain foggy. In other words, I was suffering from an anxiety hangover. Anyone who's ever suffered from a full night of anxiety attacks would know exactly how I was feeling. I took my 9 mm from my nightstand and put it back in the gun safe. I'd felt safer with it nearby but was thankful I hadn't had a reason to use it.

My house faces the west, so I peered out the window, hoping for some sunrise magic to boost my spirits. Instead, I noticed a black sedan parked at the end of my lot instead of the marked police cruiser that had been there the night before. Instantly, I recognized Reese's cinnamon-red hair on the driver's side, and it looked like Broyles in the passenger seat. They must've taken over for Jeanna and Levi sometime early this morning or last night.

My stomach twisted with a familiar unease. I hated needing a babysitter and hoped it was a whole lot of something over a whole lot of nothing.

After showering to wake up, I wore pale pink sweats and headed to the living room. As I walked through the house, I couldn't shake the feeling of being watched. The creep sending me the memories had made me feel unsafe in my own skin.

Ari sat on the couch in the living room in her rocket-ship pajamas. Her blankets and pillows were in the same pile I had left for her the night before. She was frantically scrolling through her phone, jotting down notes with her stylus.

"Come look," she said absently, waving me over.

I hadn't had my coffee yet, but the girl looked feral. Protesting might get me bitten. I walked over and stood behind her. Her phone screen resembled something out of "A Beautiful Mind," filled with ovals, branches, and sub-branches. My heart pounded, and a knot of tension tightened in my chest as I saw the chaotic web of information.

"Whatcha got there, kiddo?" I asked cautiously.

An empty cup of coffee sat on my coffee table, and Ari's hands were shaking as she held her phone up for me to see.

"Mason and I made a revenge mind map for all the people you've helped put in jail, anyone on parole, and included any family members who live in town that I could find who might hold a grudge. On top of that, I factored in any veiled threats on social media directed at you or the police."

"Mason?" I asked.

"Yeah, I hit him up to help with research. We've been DMing back and forth all night." She wagged two fingers at me. "More brains, more gains."

I didn't love that Ari had spent hours researching all my potential enemies. I loved it even less that she was able to find enough to make a whole map. I peered at her screen. "I can't believe that many people want revenge against me. It seems...excessive."

Ari tilted her head back to look up at me. "No worries, Aunt Nora." Her brown eyes were bloodshot with sleep deprivation. "We couldn't find anything with your name on it specifically prior to twenty-four hours ago, but there are a few posts from before that we think allude to you. No concrete confirmation, though."

"And in the last twenty-four hours?" I asked.

"You're better off not knowing," she answered.

I cringed. "Your answer means I definitely don't want to know."

"Sorry, I wish it was more helpful, but too much information is as bad as having too little," she said earnestly. Her speech pattern was quick and clipped, her voice rising several octaves as she went on a mini-rant. "That letter in the Gazette brought a lot of ugly out in this community and, frankly, all over the place. There are a lot of posts from people who don't live in or around Garden Cove. Heck, I found one post that originated from freaking Russia. I don't know whether to hate these people because they are the worst kind of trolls or feel sorry for them because they obviously have zero joy or love in their lives if this is how they behave toward total strangers." She sucked in a deep breath at the end. Her eyes were watery with unshed tears of her righteous indignation.

I put my hand on her shoulder. "Did you get *any* sleep last night?"

"I'm good. I've gotten less sleep studying for a final." She waved a hand dismissively. "I'm just mad as heck."

"I can tell." I squeezed her shoulder and kissed the top of her head. "Don't let the trolls win, okay? Their words can't hurt me."

"That's just it, Aunt Nora, their words can hurt." Her voice was angry. "You don't understand the reach people can get on the internet. It can damage your business and your reputation."

"I think both of those will be just fine," I said, my voice trembling slightly. "However, I'm going to need some coffee before I hear any more about all the people who hate me."

She snatched up her cup and handed it to me. "I just brewed a fresh pot," she said. "Black, two sugars."

I chuckled and shook my head as I took the mug from her, trying to hide my unease. "Coming right up." After all, the kid had worked nonstop through the night to gather data on my behalf. If she wanted to boss me around a little this morning, I would let it slide.

As I poured fresh coffee into two mugs, the doorbell rang. It startled me for a moment until I remembered that Reese and Broyles were outside watching for bad guys. She wouldn't have let anyone come to my door who wasn't on a safe list.

I hollered to Ari, "See who it is," and then finished doctoring her coffee with the two sugars.

"It's Ezra and Mason," she yelled back.

Good, I thought. Ezra loved me enough to make all the people who hated me less important. When I walked back into the living room, I expected a happier reunion, but my guy looked miserable.

"What's wrong?" I asked. "Did something else happen?"

"In a manner," he said. "The Gazette got another letter."

I set the steaming mugs on the coffee table, pushing Ari's near her phone. Worry laced through me as I thought about what another letter would do to my ability to work and live in Garden Cove. "Did they publish it?"

He shook his head. "Darla Potter put a stop to it. But that doesn't mean whoever sent it won't try to get it seen in other ways."

I clenched my jaw, wanting to scream at how easy it was for people to lie and even easier for gullible people to believe it. "Do you have it?"

"Chief Rafferty took a picture and texted it to me. It's typed and printed like the last one," he replied.

I made a gimme gesture. "Let me see."

Ezra took his phone from his pocket and pressed it to his chest. "It's bad, Nora."

"How bad is it?" I said, mimicking the classic joke style of call and respond.

Ezra didn't laugh. "Bad." He woke up his screen and handed me his phone.

What I read next made me sick to my stomach.

To the Residents of Garden Cove,

It is with a heavy heart and an even deeper sense of urgency that I write this follow-up letter. The recent events that have shaken our town to its core compel me to speak out once more. We must confront the truth about Nora Black, whose actions have proven to be a grave danger to our beloved Garden Cove.

Just a short time ago, our peaceful street fair, what should've been a grand celebration, was marred by a disruptive shooting. Panic and chaos erupted, leaving many of our friends and neighbors traumatized. While the true perpetrator remains unknown, evidence has surfaced that points to Nora Black's involvement. Her suspicious behaviors cannot be overlooked.

As if that wasn't enough, a horrifying incident at a local church has further exposed the peril she poses. She was present when a bomb, planted with malicious intent, *detonated inside the hallowed walls of Cove Community Church. Disturbing clues suggest Nora's hands, along with her psychic nose, are all over this vile act, casting an even darker shadow over her already tarnished reputation.*

Though some may find it hard to believe, the pattern of violence and terror that follows Nora Black cannot be ignored. Her presence in Garden Cove is becoming synonymous with fear and unrest. The safety of our community is at stake, and we must act decisively.

We cannot allow ourselves to be deceived by those in public law enforcement who would have you believe she's a hero. Nora Black has proven time and again that she is willing to jeopardize the lives of innocent people for her own accolades. Her cowardice, heartlessness, and now apparent involvement in these new violent crimes make her a menace we can no longer tolerate.

As concerned residents, it is our duty to protect our town from those who seek to harm it. We must demand a thorough investigation into Nora Black's activities and ensure that she is held accountable for her actions. Let us stand together, united in our resolve to restore peace and security to Garden Cove.

You'd do well to heed my Wise and Loyal council,

A Vigilant Resident

I HANDED THE PHONE BACK, feeling the blood drain from my limbs as my poor heart hammered against my chest.

"This is more than bad. It's super bad," I croaked, my voice barely above a whisper. "Nuclear bad."

"Bruh." Ari, who had been standing nearby and apparently speed-reading over my shoulder, took the phone for a closer inspection. "That's so wack. Total trash. Is this person for real?"

"Say it louder for the people in the back," Mason said as he stood beside her. "It's—"

Ezra's brow furrowed. "Real enough to write a letter and deliver it to the paper. It's a total dumpster fire."

I couldn't decipher from the letter whether the writer harbored genuine hatred towards me or if they were simply aiming to incite public outrage. Perhaps it was both. Regardless, if this went public, my reputation, as Ari had pointed out earlier, would be shredded.

"The chief is keeping the mayor away from this for now, but if it goes public, he'll have to do something to save his job," Ezra added.

"I get it," I said, feeling the weight of the situation settling in. As much as I wished Shawn could support me, he had two kids in college and hospital bills from Leila's treatments. Losing his job now would be devastating.

I heard my phone ringing from the bedroom, and I seized the opportunity to escape the living room and the offending letter. Glancing at the caller ID, I saw it was Pippa, so I answered immediately.

"Hello, good morning," I said, attempting to sound composed despite feeling anything but. "What's up?"

"I hate to call because I know you have a lot on your plate, but someone broke a back window at the shop," she said.

"How?" I asked, my mind racing.

"A good old-fashioned brick," she replied.

My stomach burned, and I worried I was developing an ulcer. "How come the security company didn't notify us?"

"I don't know. Our alarm is wireless, so there was no power to cut, but it's been smashed to pieces."

Ezra entered the bedroom, concern etched on his face. "Did something happen?"

"Someone broke a window at the shop with a brick, and then they demolished our security system," I explained.

"A smash and crash," Ezra remarked grimly.

I shook my head in disbelief. "Tell me more." I put Pippa on speaker. "I have Ezra here. He's calling this a smash and crash."

"That's where thieves will break into a place and smash the alarm before it can be triggered. Usually, there's a ten to fifteen-second delay to give owners time to turn off the alarm before the security company is alerted. A lot of security systems bank on burglars being too stupid to figure it out."

"Son-of-a-birch tree," Pippa grumbled.

"Did anything get stolen?" I asked, anxiety gnawing at me.

"Not that I can see, but you have a lot of stock in the

back, and I can't tell if any is missing or not. I took the money home with me yesterday. After the craziness in the street, I didn't want to risk leaving it in the shop over the weekend."

"Good idea," I reassured her. "I'll be down in a little bit to check things out."

Ezra shook his head emphatically, his worry mirroring mine. It wasn't going to stop me from going, though.

"I called the police," Pippa informed us. "I figured we should make a report."

"Sounds good. See you soon." I ended the call and turned to Ezra. "Is this the work of our guy or some disgruntled citizen who doesn't like having a nosy psychic in their town?"

"If it is the guy, I'm sure he left you some kind of clue," Ezra said, wrapping his arms around me tightly. "Whatever it is, we'll find it out together."

THIRTEEN

The drive to Scents and Scentsability felt endless. Ezra had let Reese know what was going on before driving me in his truck to the shop. Not driving had left my brain free reign to conjure up a thousand scenarios of what this jerk had planned for me next, each more disturbing than the last. I couldn't shake the feeling that the person who had been taunting me and putting everyone I cared about in danger had finally taken things a step further.

When we arrived, Ezra parked haphazardly in front of the building. There was another police car out front, and I opened his truck door and was out before he could cut the engine.

Inside the shop, the mingled scents of essential oils and floral perfumes filled the air but brought me no comfort. I heard voices in the back and fast-walked through the door that opened to my workshop. Large pieces of glass were on the concrete floor, and the window next to the alley door had a huge gaping hole. But that's not what stopped me in my tracks. My work-shop...no, my sanctuary, had been violated. There was nothing obvious. No stools had been overturned, my cutting table was clear of debris, and the metal drying racks filled with my patriotic soaps were undisturbed.

Pippa was talking to Jeanna Treece and her partner Levi.

"Hey, Jeanna." I mirrored her words from yesterday. "We have to stop meeting like this."

She smiled genially. "I drew the short stick for the holiday weekend," she said. "'Fraid you're stuck with me."

"I'll take you any day." Frankly, I was glad Jeanna and her partner had been scheduled for the holiday weekend. I knew her and Levi well enough to trust them, and my trust was in short supply right now.

A half a minute later, Ezra joined us. "I have Reese and Broyles checking out the alley," he said as he knelt by the bashed alarm system.

He inspected the damage. "Yep, as I suspected. They smashed it before it could go off."

Pippa's face was pale and drawn. "Nora, I'm so sorry. I should've checked out different security systems. This wasn't cheap, but it also wasn't super expensive. This is my fault."

A few years ago, when several businesses were getting burgled, Pippa had the alarm installed. It looked like the only thing keeping someone from breaking in had been the stickers they gave us to put on the doors.

"You didn't force this jerk to break into the place," I told her. "He's the only one at fault." I tried to give her a reassuring look, but it was hard when all I felt was violated and vulnerable. "It's okay, Pip. We'll figure this out."

Levi moved around us, taking photos and dusting for fingerprints.

I looked at my drying racks again, and something felt...off. There wasn't any empty space. It was full the way I'd left it, and yet... "Look," I pointed. "There's a pure blue soap in there." The others were red, white, and blue, so I hadn't noticed it at first. "I didn't put that there."

"You sure?" Ezra said.

"I'm one hundred percent positive," I assured him. "There should be another red, white, and blue soap there. It's all from the same batches."

Levi, who was wearing gloves, walked over to the rack to check it out. "It's a darker blue than your other soaps, too," he said. "More blueberry blue than Old Glory blue." He sniffed. "And it smells different."

"The Red, White, and Blue soaps should smell like strawberries, blueberries, and sweet vanilla cream," I told him. "What does the other smell like?"

He looked back at me. "It smells like wintergreen mints."

"Wintergreen?" I didn't have any methyl salicylate,

the chemical used to create wintergreen flavor and scent, so it hadn't been made in my workshop. "Whoever put that on the rack wanted me to find it."

"I think we all know who that someone is," Jeanna said.

"The Scent Stalker," Levi announced.

"The who?" Ezra asked with alarm.

Levi's face reddened as he suddenly found his rubber gloves interesting to look at. Finally, he met Ezra's gaze. "Sorry, Detective Holden. It's the term a few of us have taken to calling this guy. It sort of stuck."

"I swear if that name ends up in the newspaper, someone is going to end up on an extended leave," Ezra threatened.

"Yes, sir," Levi said quickly. "Heard." He pointed at the soap. "Should we bag it?"

"Not yet," I interjected. "I have to smell it."

"It's what the guy wants," Pippa said. "Don't give him the satisfaction."

"I wish it was that easy," I told her. "But he's already made a plan, and if I don't at least try and figure it out, someone might get hurt. I can't live with that on my conscience."

"Whatever that man does is his fault, not yours," she told me, throwing my words back in my face.

I smiled. "I see what you did there."

She winked. "It was good advice."

"Nora's right," Ezra said. "Her avoiding the vision

isn't going to stop the...uhm, this guy from pulling off whatever dumbass thing he has planned for today."

"Scent Stalker," Pippa whispered as if taking the moniker out for a test drive. "Does it really fit, though?" She squinted as she thought about it for half a second. "How about the Fragrance Phantom, the Perfumed Prowler, or," she snapped her fingers as if excited by the idea. "The Scented Shadow."

"Don't encourage them," Ezra groaned.

"Besides, those sound like old radio shows from the nineteen twenties."

"Is that the sort of thing you listened to growing up?" Levi asked.

I gave him a scathing stare. "I used to like you."

Levi chuckled. "Just kidding."

"Can I put him on an extended leave?" I asked Ezra.

He shook his head. "Not unless you take my job." He switched his gaze to Levi. "But that doesn't mean I won't do it for you."

"And that's why I love you," I told him.

He grinned. "I hope that's not the only reason."

I flushed and gave him an eye roll. "We'll discuss all the reasons later. Right now, I should smell that soap. Who knows, maybe I won't see anything."

"We can always hope," Pippa said.

"Officer Walters," Ezra ordered. "Get the soap for Ms. Black so she doesn't contaminate the evidence."

I hadn't been planning on handling the soap bar, but

I let it slide. Levi had gloves on, so I was happy to let him hold it.

He carefully picked up the bar and held it out. I felt weird sniffing something in his hand, but a psychic girl had to do what a psychic girl had to do.

The strong odor of menthol, wintergreen, and eucalyptus emanated from the soap, and I focused all my energy on trying to block out all the other scents in the workshop. I inhaled deeply once more and felt a slight burning in my nostrils, then...

A person dressed entirely in blue—a blue hoodie, blue rubber gloves, and a full plastic Captain America Halloween mask—stands amidst the concrete walls of the dimly lit room. It reminds me of the same place where the popcorn memory was created. The air is thick with the scent of menthol, eucalyptus, and wintergreen, strong enough to clear out someone's sinuses.

The mysterious maniac stirs the contents of the bowl with purpose, the glass clink of a stirring rod against the sides. Next to the bowl is a white silicone soap mold, its surface smooth and unblemished, ready to receive the liquid concoction. There are some bottles of clear liquids, their labels obscured in the dim light. What is he adding? He's careful as he uses a glass dropper to add more ingredients to the mix.

As he finishes his witches' brew, he adds five drops of blue food coloring and two bars of amber-colored soap. His movements are deliberate and precise as if he's orchestrating some dark symphony. The color transforms into a vivid blueberry blue, and the menthol scent intensifies.

Then, in a voice distorted by his voice changer, he speaks with chilling confidence, mimicking the unique force of nature that is Jennifer Coolidge's tone: "Light up the sky like the fourth of July. I'm coming in hot, dog, and the race is on. Wow, wow. Try an' stop me. I'm unstoppable. Stop, drop, and roll, hero, or let it burn, baby, burn."

The words send a shiver down my spine. I hear two clangs, like a clock striking. Captain America, with a muffled voice that is distinctly male, mutters, "Well, shee-it."

Emerging from the vision, my breath caught in my throat, excitement tingling through my veins like an electric current. "He slipped up. He thinks he's clever, but he's finally made a mistake."

"Oh, damn it, that burns!" Levi exclaimed, his voice sharp with pain, then he fumbled and dropped the soap. His latex gloves, now riddled with holes, revealed skin turning an alarming shade of brown. "What is this?"

Jeanna, also gloved, instinctively reached for the dropped evidence. Broyles, who must've entered while I was in the midst of my vision, intervened swiftly. "Don't touch it. Not with gloves on," he cautioned, eyeing Levi's hand. "Get that washed off." His gaze flicked to me. "Do you have any baking soda?"

"There might be some in the fridge. I use it to neutralize odors," I hurriedly replied as Broyles dashed to the fridge. "What caused the burn on his hand?"

"If I had to guess, it's nitric acid," Broyles explained. "It eats through latex fast. The brown discoloration on the skin is a dead giveaway. Levi's lucky it wasn't fuming nitric acid. That stuff bursts into flames upon contact with latex."

"I don't feel lucky," Levi gritted out, his hand held under the rushing water in my sink. "It feels anything but."

The clear liquid the masked man had been so careful to concoct must've been nitric acid. Was that the 'burn, baby, burn' clue?

Jeanna interjected, "I've called an ambulance."

"I don't need an ambulance," Levi protested through clenched teeth, then winced. "Ow, ow."

Broyles retrieved a two-pound bag of baking soda from the fridge and began pouring it over Levi's drenched hand. After a few moments, he asked, "Feeling any better?"

Levi gripped his hand firmly, then uttered, "It's not worsening."

"Good." Broyles gave Levi a hearty pat on the shoulder. "Keep it under running water until the paramedic arrives."

"Quick thinking, Broyles. Well done," Ezra commended. "How do we contain the caustic substance? And is there a risk of explosion? If I remember correctly, nitric acid and glycerin combine to form nitroglycerin, right?"

Broyles chuckled. "Not without sulfuric acid. And truthfully, if it were nitro, it would've blown up when Levi dropped it on the hard floor." My eyes widened at the revelation. "Yep, kaboom. Enough to wipe us all out."

I winced. "Glad to have dodged that."

"Butyl rubber gloves or some other tool should be safe for handling it," Broyles instructed Ezra. "And we can transport it in a glass dish."

"I'll leave the specifics to you," Ezra deferred.

The soap's composition lingered in my mind, one ingredient away from one of the most volatile explosives. Nitroglycerin required minimal provocation to detonate. You didn't need to be a demolition expert to grasp the gravity of the situation or its potential lethality.

Had the Scented Stalker, as Levi dubbed him, attempted to produce nitroglycerin and failed? The attention-seeking lunatic spoke of illuminating the sky like the Fourth of July. If he had indeed created such a large quantity, it would've been catastrophic for us all.

"Nora, you mentioned he made an error," Ezra interjected. "What did you witness?"

"It was him," I recounted, "dressed entirely in blue this time, sporting blue rubber gloves and a Captain America mask. He was mimicking Jennifer Coolidge and said, 'Light up the sky like the fourth of July. I'm coming in hot, dog, and the race is on. Wow, wow. Try an' stop me. I'm unstoppable. Stop, drop, and roll, hero, or let it burn, baby, burn.' All while making the soap."

"Isn't 'stop, drop, and roll' from 'Legally Blonde'?" Pippa, who had been unusually quiet, chimed in.

"It's bend and snap," Broyles corrected, looking sheepish. "I have a friend who's a fan of the 'Legally Blonde' movies."

Reese entered. "Any potential evidence in the alley has been collected and sent to the station." She surveyed the room, puzzled. "What did I miss?"

"Apparently, Jennifer Coolidge tried to blow us all up," Pippa said, simplifying the events while exaggerating them.

"Not Jennifer Coolidge." Reese's brow furrowed, forming a deep crease. "I adored her in 'Legally Blonde.'"

Jeanna and I exchanged knowing glances. A smirk played at the corner of her mouth.

Ezra cleared his throat, redirecting the conversation. "Where did he go wrong, Nora?"

"There was a chiming, more like a clang, in the background, like an old clock striking two," I recalled. "I don't think he expected me to hear it, because when the clock chimed, he muttered, 'Well, shee-it,' sounding like a man. Muffled, but definitely male."

"Would you recognize it if you heard it again?" Ezra inquired.

"He had a mask on, so I'm uncertain. I didn't recognize it during the vision."

"It's not much," Broyles acknowledged.

"But it's a lead," I insisted. "At least now we know our suspect is male."

"White and over forty," I added.

Ezra met my gaze. "How did you determine that?"

"Ari deduced it," I explained. "She said anyone born after nineteen ninety wouldn't have used EZ Reader as a clue. They'd have used God from 'Bruce Almighty'."

"Valid point," Levi agreed. "I would've gone with his character from the Dark Knight trilogy."

"I know him from 'The Bucket List,'" Jeanna contributed.

"Regardless, white male, over forty," I reaffirmed.

"Fantastic," Reese remarked dryly. "That narrows it down to about a thousand guys in Garden Cove."

"Including me," Broyles confessed. "Just hit forty. Although, in my defense, I have no idea who EZ Reader is."

I was eager to conclude this discussion before I got labeled a Boomer again. "What about the other stuff? Do you think he was talking about the soap?" Because I didn't think so. Something told me the nitric acid was a warning, a prelude to something much bigger. This wasn't just revenge for this psychopath. He was enjoying the game and was playing to win at any cost.

FOURTEEN

Pippa packed up and headed to Moo-La-lattes to meet Tippi and the kids shortly after the paramedics arrived for Levi. I was glad she went. I would worry less knowing she was with Jordy and her family. It had taken a few hours, but the police thoroughly searched the shop front and back to ensure that my nemesis had not left any more caustic gifts lying around for me. Thankfully, the place was clean. When they began to clear out of the store with their equipment in tow, I stepped out front for some fresh air.

That's when I saw Carol Billingsly, the editor of the Garden Cove Gazette, interviewing people across the street from the shop. Carol, an attractive woman in her fifties with sandy blonde hair and a professional appearance, had been responsible for the anonymous letter getting published in the paper, and now she was speaking with Mr. Lems in front of my store. And she had a camera guy with her. Anger boiled inside me, but I wasn't about to let it be immortalized on film. Still, I couldn't believe Mr. Lems had agreed to be recorded. I bet the old sourpuss was giving her an earful about me.

I spotted his son Waylon, standing under the awning of his father's shop. When he met my gaze, he had the good sense to look embarrassed. I stormed over to him.

"Why is your dad talking to a reporter?" I demanded.

"Hello to you too, Nora," he replied. "Sorry, but I'm not in charge of my dad today."

I felt a twinge of embarrassment for being rude. Waylon had always been nice, unlike his dad. "I sincerely apologize. I haven't had a lot of sleep, but that's no reason to take it out on you."

He glanced at the cop cars and the ambulance parked along the street. "What's going on with your place?"

"We got broken into last night," I explained. "The police are investigating."

Waylon's eyes widened. "Man, that's terrible. Did they steal much?"

I shook my head. "I'm not sure anything was taken at this point." Except for the bar of soap the guy removed to replace it with the nitric acid one, I thought.

He glanced back at his dad's furniture store. "Maybe I should get an alarm system put on Dad's store. But it's hard to justify the monthly payments for a store that's only open during the summer and only three days a week."

"I get that," I sympathized. "We had an alarm system, and it did jack to prevent getting burgled."

"Huh," he grunted. "Bad luck. There's been a lot of that going around lately."

Edgar Jones, his arm still slung, was stopped by Carol as he walked past her interview with Mr. Lems. He shook his head vigorously, to the effect of saying "no comment." Poor Edgar. The man had been put through it yesterday. I hoped he was taking care of his injury. He put his head down and kept walking.

Waylon tipped his head to me. "Welp, I gotta get going. People to do, work to see."

I groaned at his attempt at humor, and he laughed.

"Are you leaving?" I asked.

"Yeah, there's not much to help Dad with today, and it's Sunday."

"Okay," I said, absently watching Carol gesticulate toward my shop while she talked to Mr. Lems. They were far enough away that I couldn't tell what she was asking, but I imagined it had to do with me.

"You really don't like that reporter," he observed.

"That woman hates me," I murmured. "And I'm beginning to hate her back."

"Why does she hate you?" Waylon asked.

"I have no idea," I replied honestly. Any theories I had were all speculation.

"Maybe you should ask her then. You know, carpe the diem."

"That's a good idea," I told him.

He grinned. "I get those every once in a while."

I smiled. "Your dad might not tell you this, but you're a good son, Waylon. I hope Mr. Lems knows how lucky he is to have you helping him."

"Nah, I just do some odds and ends and help him keep the lights on. Besides, he lets me put some of my sculptures up for sale in the store. Can't say it would hurt my feelings if he sold the shop before the bank decides to take it. There's been a few offers, but my dad's stubborn. Even so, he's had a tough go of it lately, so I've been trying to help him out as much as I can when I have time off from my day job. Dad's got back pain nowadays and can't do a lot of things he used to. I guess it's the price of getting old." He shrugged. "But better than the alternative, am I right?"

"Right." I'd taken care of my mother for two years when she was diagnosed with cancer, and even in the hardest of times during her cancer treatments and the last few months when we knew the end was coming, I was grateful I could be there for her. I hoped it was like that for Waylon with his dad. Mr. Lems wasn't an easy man to be around, and it had to be even harder for his son. "I'm sorry again for my poor excuse for manners."

Before he could respond, I saw Carol signal the camera guy to pack up. Then, she shook hands with Mr.

Lems. With the camera off, I took the opportunity to confront her.

"Carpe diem," I said to Waylon as my parting words, then made a beeline for the irritating reporter. I passed Mr. Lems, who scowled at me as he crossed the street to return to his shop.

"What have you got against me?" I asked her point-blank the moment I got across the street. "Why are you coming after me like this?"

"You're nuts," Carol said, folding her arms. "How am I coming after you?"

"First, you print that damning anonymous letter, and now you're interviewing neighboring businesses about me. How would you describe it?"

Carol laughed loudly. "First, I thought the letter was a hoot. It's an anonymous letter claiming a prominent businesswoman is a psychic. It's not hard news. I thought it would give people a laugh. Secondly, I'm not here interviewing people about you. The mayor is giving a press conference at the grandstand pavilion in front of the courthouse at noon about the false alarm shooting at the fair yesterday and the stink bomb that was set off at the Community Cove Church. Channel Five in Kansas City reached out and asked me if I could cover it for them. I'm out here interviewing Garden Cove citizens, trying to get some color commentary to add to the reel." She jabbed a finger at me. "It's not about you, Nora. This could be my big break. The thing that gets me out of this Podunk town. I've been trying to leave for over thirty years, and you're not going to ruin it for me by making false accusations. Not this time. Not again!"

Again? She acted as if the reason she was in Garden Cove was my fault. "How did I ruin—"

"I don't owe you any explanations." She cut me off. "This conversation is over."

"Hey, hey." Ezra held his hands out in front of him and patted the air as if he could tamp down the explosive energy brewing as he walked over. "Why don't you just move along?" he suggested to Carol. "The mayor is speaking from the bandstand. That's four blocks east of here."

"Freedom of the press," Carol retorted snidely. "The First Amendment gives me the right to express, publish, and share information, ideas, and opinions without fear of censorship or government interference," she recited. "And in my opinion, which I'm legally allowed to have, your girlfriend sucks." She stuck her tongue out at me.

Ezra stepped between us, mostly to keep me from lunging at the total witch with a capital B. "Settle down."

"Real mature," I said to Carol. I'm sure she'd feel the sting of my comeback for days. Not.

She smirked. "It takes one to know one." With a flourish, she turned around and walked away.

I was stunned. "What's that supposed to mean?"

"It means you probably shouldn't be starting fights on the street where anyone can record it," Ezra replied.

"The camera was off."

"That one was, but..." He gazed around the streets, and I saw a couple of people with their phones out. "The streets have eyes and ears."

"I hate technology." I crossed my arms with disdain. "Besides, I don't suck. Progress sucks."

He sniffed and, with all seriousness, said, "Because you're in a bad mood, I'm not going to mention that it doesn't bother me one bit when you occasionally suck."

"Now you're being nasty." I tried not to smile, but my damn lips betrayed me. "Stop being cute. I'm mad as hell, and that's the way I want to stay."

"You go ahead and be mad." He gestured to my shop. "You've earned the right."

"Levi's back," I noted.

"He got back from the hospital about ten minutes ago."

The paramedics had taken him to the hospital, at Ezra's insistence, to get checked out. The young officer's hand was bandaged up, and he was talking to Reese on the sidewalk. He must've been superficial if they released him.

"How's his hand?" I asked, wanting verification.

Ezra looked up, his expression calm and professional. "He'll be all right. The doctor said he was lucky. The baking soda Broyles used neutralized the nitric acid before it could do any real damage. If Levi hadn't been wearing gloves, he probably wouldn't have gotten burned at all. I guess nitric acid has a strong reaction to latex."

I stared at Levi for a moment, taking in his defiant stance and the tension in his shoulders as he continued his conversation with his superior. He'd gotten lucky. We all had. Every situation this madman put us in could've gone seriously wrong. His dangerous antics were juvenile in nature and a bit geeky.

I turned to Ezra as the thought marinated in my mind. "The man doing this has dropped bullets in a hot pan to make them explode, mixed sulfur powder with sugar and lit it up to create a stink bomb, and mixed nitric acid into glycerin to make a soap that would cause burns if handled with latex gloves. Don't these sound like science experiments? Like the kind you see on television or watch your teacher perform out on the lawn?"

Ezra, standing with his arms crossed, nodded thoughtfully. "But he couldn't have known the soap would be handled with gloves."

"Couldn't he?" I shook my head, frustration creeping into my tone. "He made sure that we knew the building was broken into by throwing a brick through the window and smashing my security system. He had to know that once I noticed the out-of-place soap, it would be collected as evidence. What gets worn when evidence is collected? Gloves." I gave Ezra a sharp look. "I bet he thought I'd be the one wearing the gloves since I would have to get close enough to the soap to smell it."

Ezra's brow furrowed as he considered my words. "You might be on to something."

"But what? All I've demonstrated is that The

Scented Stalker is probably a Bill Nye, the Science Guy, fan." My exasperation was real and kind of loud.

"Stop saying that." Ezra whipped his head around, looking for nearby bystanders. "What if someone overhears?"

"About the guy liking Bill Nye?"

"No," Ezra whispered urgently. "The Scented Stalker." His lip curled in distaste. "I don't want the press getting a hold of it because that's a name that won't go away."

I made a face, unable to suppress a slight grin. "It's catchy."

"Extremely," Ezra agreed. "And it's the last thing the department needs right now. So..." He mimicked locking his lips and throwing away the key.

I did the same, hoping I didn't accidentally pick the lock and slip up later.

"Hey," Ezra said, his tone shifting to business. "I was looking for you because I got a call from the chief. When we're done here, I have to move my team down to the grandstand on the courthouse lawn for the mayor's speech. Chief wants all available officers on hand working security, just in case."

"In case?" I asked, raising an eyebrow.

"It's his boss," Ezra said with a smirk.

"And he's yours," I replied.

Ezra smiled, his green eyes softening as he looked at me. "Now you're getting it."

I reached out, brushing a stray lock of hair from his forehead. "Be careful, okay?"

"Always." Ezra took my hand, squeezing it gently. "I'll leave Treece and Walters with you."

"But Shawn wants all available officers..."

He dipped his head, his lips grazing mine for a brief moment. "Until we catch this guy, Treece and Walters are unavailable officers." He brushed my jawline with his thumb. "You'll stay out of trouble."

"I make no promises," I went up on my tiptoes, leaning in for a quick kiss. "But I'll try."

"I guess that'll have to do," Ezra chuckled. "If you find anything else..."

"I'll call you first."

"Correct answer," he said, his voice alight with amusement.

Reese began to wave in our direction then she jogged across the street to meet us. "Hey, Boss. We just got fingerprints back from that coin you found yesterday behind the florist shop."

"Yeah? Did we get a match?"

Reese pursed her lips. "We sure did." She shook her head as if in disbelief. "It was a full thumb and a partial index finger match to Edgar Jones."

"Edgar?" I couldn't believe it. "He was injured in the blast. He's the victim."

"Or is he," Reese countered. "It's awfully convenient he just happened to be present at the street fair incident and the Cove Community Church bombing," she added. "I don't think so."

Ezra swore. "Get an APB out on the man. Let's track him down."

"He's here," I informed them. "I saw him walking past Carol earlier when she was interviewing Mr. Lems."

"Which way was he heading?" Ezra asked.

I pointed east. "That way."

Reese's hand went to the radio on her belt. "Toward the courthouse."

"The mayor's address will be starting soon," Ezra said. "Call in the team. We need everyone down there now to find Edgar Jones."

"What do you think he's planning to do?" The mayor had just arranged to speak to the press and the memory had been planted before Edgar would've known it was happening. This wasn't right, I thought. Nothing about this felt right.

FIFTEEN

"Come on," I urged Jeanna, feeling a twinge of impatience. "I don't need a babysitter."

"Aww, but I'm the best babysitter in town," she quipped, her eyes sparkling with mischief. "Just ask Levi."

"Har har," her partner muttered, flexing the fingers on his bandaged hand with a grimace.

"Fine," I conceded. "But if I have to sit around, I'm going to need caffeine." The few sips of coffee I'd had early that morning were wearing thin. "We can at least go to the coffee shop, right?"

My reluctant agreement earned a nod, and soon enough, we were making our way to Moo-La-Lattes. Before we went inside, Jeanna cautioned me, "I know your friends are in there, but no talking about Jones. Not until we have him in custody, okay?"

"No talking about Edgar." I crossed my heart but didn't hope to die.

This wasn't that kind of promise. The more I thought about it, the more Edgar made sense, but I didn't see any connection to him and any of the prior cases I had worked for the Garden Cove PD. He was certainly the right age, sex, and race to be the culprit, but I needed the why of it to understand. I only hoped they caught him before he did anything destructive.

When we strolled into Moo-La-Lattes, the scents of coffee, chai, caramel, chocolate, and vanilla clung to the air like a dessert paradise. The aromas always brought on a deluge of memories, but luckily, I rarely saw the same memories twice.

"Nora!" Pippa waved at me from a table near the back, her smile broad and welcoming. Tippi sat next to her, JJ was in a booster seat, and JP was happily bouncing in his bouncy chair at her feet. She gestured to the seat across from her. "Everything wrapped up at the shop?"

"Yep," I told her. "We can get back in there now, but let's leave it until tomorrow." I didn't have the heart to work today, not with everything going on. "Hey, on the bright side, I've grown two extra heads," I replied, using my thumbs to indicate Jeanna and Levi.

"We can push two tables together," Jordy suggested, his voice warm and inviting. "So, you all can sit together."

I flashed him a grateful look. "Thanks, Jordy. You're the best."

He laughed. "I won't tell Easy you said so." Today, his long hair was pulled back in a Viking-style braid, and he wore a tight black t-shirt with a line drawing of a French cow sporting a beret and the words "Moo-La-Lattes" in a speech bubble. He noticed me looking. "Do you like it?"

"It's adorable," I said with a grin. "Where's mine?"

He grinned back, nodding toward Pippa's table. "Talk to my marketing manager."

"Are you moonlighting on me?" I teased her, raising an eyebrow.

"Not hardly," she scoffed, a playful glint in her eyes. "That creation is all Tippi."

Her younger sister grinned, her face awash with pleasure. "It was just for fun. I used to love art in high school, so I decided to take a graphic art class for my art requirement. I really enjoyed doing it."

"And art is great therapy," Pippa added, a note of pride in her voice. "Tippi's going to be a great counselor."

I saw a fleeting wistful look cross Tippi's face, her smile faltering for just a moment.

Levi and Jeanna worked to push the tables together, then sat down in the seats closest to the door.

Tippi, who loved to flirt with everyone, pressed her fingertips against her chest, drawing attention to her vneck t-shirt. She leaned in and asked, "Are we in danger?"

Levi and Jeanna both glanced over, their eyes lingering. I tried not to snicker, but it wasn't easy. Tippi had a great body and excellent breasts. I couldn't blame them for looking.

Jordy brought a tray of drinks to the table, his smile never wavering. "One frozen chai latte for Nora, a mocha Frappuccino for m'lady, a double-shot espresso caramel macchiato for the artist, and two Americanos for the cops: one black with four sugars, the other with cream, no sugar." He handed out the beverages with a flourish. "Is everyone good?"

"Perfect for me," I said, inhaling the spicy aroma with a contented sigh. "Heaven."

"Thanks, Jordy," Jeanna said, her eyes lighting up as she took the Americano with heavy cream and no sugar. Levi accepted the other one with a nod.

"So," Tippi said eagerly. "Tell us what's going on. Pippa said the bomb at the church wasn't a real bomb. What the heck was it then? The smell was disgusting. It took me five washes to get the odor out of my hair."

I glanced a Jeanna for permission, and she shrugged. "It's not a secret. The mayor's planning to tell the whole town in about..." She looked at the digital clock behind the coffee bar. "...ten minutes."

"Oh, good." Tippi rubbed her hands together. "We're getting the scoop early."

"It was a homemade stink bomb." I fanned my hand

in front of my nose. "Apparently, if you add sulfur powder with sugar and ignite it with gunpowder, it creates a disgustingly putrid gas."

"Sulfur dioxide," Jeanna said. "That's the gas it makes, and it stinks to high heaven."

"So we weren't in any real danger," Pippa mused.

"That's not the case," Levi jumped in. "If you inhale a large concentration of sulfur dioxide, it's toxic, plus, when the bomb went off, shrapnel from the container was embedded in the walls. That could have seriously injured someone."

Tippi drew her finger in a circle on the table in front of Levi. "You're a seriously serious person, aren't you, Officer Walters?"

I almost choked on my frozen chai when I laughed while trying to take a sip. The bomb might not have killed anyone, but Tippi's flirting might.

Levi shifted in his chair, his expression waffling between flattered and scared. I didn't blame him. Tippi was beautiful, like her sister, but she was also headstrong and fierce as well. I imagined any guy who ended up with her would have to accept that she was the boss of them.

"Anyhow," I said, rescuing Levi. "To summarize, it was a stink bomb, but not the harmless kind you find in a joke shop."

"Who in the world would have those chemicals on hand? I mean, if someone put in a big order, wouldn't they be easy to trace?" Pippa asked.

"Pharmacy companies, demolition experts, farms, manufacturers, labs, and gold miners," Levi rattled off.

"Gold miners?" Pippa asked. "What would they use it for?"

"I'm not an expert," Levi said. "Just good at Googling. From what I skimmed, it can clean and purify the gold."

"They used to use mercury," I added. "To clean gold, I mean."

"That sounds dangerous," Tippi commented.

"No more dangerous than the acids," he replied. There was a glint in his eye that I interpreted as interest. Maybe Officer Walters didn't need nor want to be saved.

Good for him, and good for Tippi. Levi, from what I knew, was a decent enough man, and after three years of sobriety, Tippi was more than ready for dating.

"Burt Adler," Pippa exclaimed. "He was a pharmacist. What if it's someone who is getting revenge for him?"

"Not pharmacist," Levi corrected. "The pharmaceutical companies. The ones who make the drugs. And, while Burt was pushing drugs through his business, he wasn't making them."

"Since there isn't a farm anywhere near Garden Cove, we can rule that out," Jordy said as he came back with a pot of coffee and topped off Jeanna and Levi's cups.

I wanted to shout to the room, "They have a suspect!

We can quit guessing!" but I'd promised Jeanna I'd keep my trap shut.

Jeanna put her phone on the table. "The Gazette is going live with the mayor's speech now. Do we want to watch?"

Did I want to hear or see Carol Billingsly? No. But I did want to hear what the mayor had to say. "Sure," I groused. "Let's watch, but I'd appreciate the volume lowered until the mayor comes on."

"You got it," Jeanna said. "Nobody wants to hear that windbag, anyways."

"Carol or the mayor?" I asked.

"You got me there." Jeanna barked a laugh. "It's a coin flip."

JP began to fuss. "I feel the same way, Jordy, Jr," I told my godson. I reached down and unlatched him from the bouncy chair, picked him up and began to bounce the sweet boy on my knee. JJ squealed with delight as her baby brother vibrated right in front of her eyes. She was still at that age where object permanence wasn't a thing, so when he was on the floor, she'd probably thought he'd disappeared. My picking him up was like magic to her.

"He's probably getting hungry," Pippa said.

"I'll make him a bottle," Jordy said, grabbing the diaper bag and taking it behind the bar.

Jeanna turned the volume up on her phone with the camera zoomed in on Allison Green.

Mayor Green stood resolutely at the grandstand

outside the courthouse, her auburn hair catching the afternoon sunlight.

"Good evening, citizens of Garden Cove," Mayor Green began, her voice projecting through the speakers of Jeanna's phone. "I understand there has been concern over the incidents this Memorial Weekend. Let me assure you that the reported shooting at the street fair was a false alarm. A harmless prank perpetrated by a disruptive sort. There was no danger to the public at any time."

The crowd around the grandstand murmured doubtful exchanges. I glanced at my friends, knowing we shared the same reservations. Edgar had been injured by shrapnel from the kettle—not exactly harmless, even if he was the one responsible.

"The bomb scare at the church was also baseless," Mayor Green continued, her tone firm. "It was a stink bomb, intended to cause panic without posing any real danger. Our police force responded promptly, prioritizing public safety."

"Hah!" I scowled. JP reached up, tapped me on the cheek, blew a bubble, then flashed me a big toothless grin. Using baby talk and addressing the three-month-old, I said, "Mayor Green wouldn't even think about shutting down her precious fundraiser." She seemed more concerned about votes than public safety.

Mayor Green added, "Our officers are actively investigating both incidents and we expect to make an arrest soon."

My fingers tapped nervously on the table. I had spent the weekend piecing together clues and trying to make sense of it all. The threat to myself and my friends seemed far from ending.

"And I want to reassure everyone," Mayor Green intoned, "that Garden Cove remains a safe and welcoming community. Our tourism industry is crucial to our economy, and we won't allow these incidents to deter us." She raised her fist in the air. "You can trust in our police and local government to do their best for you." She gave the group a broad smile. "Go Green with Green!"

As the speech concluded, there was a smattering of applause from the crowd in front of the courthouse, but it was clear the citizens of Garden Cove weren't convinced.

My friends and I exchanged solemn looks. "She's full of hot air," I said with a lively tone. I finished by tapping my godson on the nose. "Isn't that right, JP? Yes, it is. She's full of nonsense." He grinned again, his face turning red as his smile widened. "Uh oh. That's not sulfur gas," I joked before handing him quickly to his mom. "Aunt Nora is not on diaper duty."

She chuckled and loudly said, "Jordy, come get your boy. He's left you a surprise."

I glanced at Jeanna's phone. She turned the volume down as Carol finished her report on the event. I spotted Ezra swiftly moving in the background. Reese and Broyles appeared on screen from the other side.

"Hey, there's Easy," Tippi exclaimed. "What's he—"

Allison Green screamed and stumbled away from her podium as a man holding his arm ran up the steps to the grandstand, his face as red as JP's had been, sheer panic in his eyes as the camera zoomed in on him. The mayor's people surrounded her for protection while Ezra tackled the man, grabbing his legs and bringing him down, while Reese climbed over him and slapped the cuffs on. Several people in the crowd cheered louder for the arrest than they had for the mayor's speech.

"Oh my God," Pippa said. "Is that our banker?"

"Yep," I confirmed. "That's Edgar."

Still, something didn't sit right with me. I'd been with Edgar in that booth after his injury. He'd been genuinely scared, and the entire time we were together, I didn't see him with popcorn. The evidence my point in his direction, but I didn't buy it. Something was foul in Garden Cove, and it wasn't just JP's diaper.

CHAPTER
SIXTEEN

They'd built a new police station in Garden Cove about five years back. When Gilly was arrested, it was the first time I had stepped foot in the place since my dad passed away. I thought going to the station would bring up too many painful memories, but it was the opposite. It looked completely different from the old building, so I found I had no emotional attachment to the place whatsoever.

The same couldn't be said now. This was where my sweetheart worked, and I had spent a lot of time inside these walls assisting with cases. The cops inside were once again like family to me. If I had to give it up, I'd miss it. Unfortunately, if my character continued to be smeared in public, I might not have a choice. I'd be a liability for cases going to trial, not an asset.

Shawn had called me shortly after the arrest and

summoned me to the police station. He said that Mayor Green wanted a word with me, and he didn't make it sound like a good thing. However, I didn't go running there like a lapdog being called to its master. I was still in my pale pink sweats, and there was no way on this "Green" earth that I was going to meet with the Mayor looking like I was on a trek to the grocery store.

Instead, I went home, showered, and changed into something that would give the mayor pause before she came at me. I'd worked as a corporate leader for years, and I knew how to pull off a power suit. I picked a tan linen blazer and wore a chocolate brown vest beneath it. The vest was fitted, like my slacks, and didn't require a shirt under it. My arms were decently fit, even at fifty-six, and I wanted to be able to show them off with a casual drop of the jacket if needed. I chose a pair of Gucci signature mules. The chunky heel made walking easier and standing for long periods tolerable. I tucked my hair into a bun and pinned it with a diamond hairpin that had been my mother's, making sure my makeup was appropriate for daytime but added a touch of bronzer for a bit of glam.

I was going to give Allison Green the take-no-prisoners, ball-busting, deal-sealing Nora Black, who knew how to get things done.

When I walked into the station, Broyles was the first person I encountered. He assessed me up and down and then said, "Day-um. You did not come to play."

"I did not," I agreed.

"You can relax a minute," he informed me as he scratched his head. He'd said earlier that he'd just turned forty. In the god-awful fluorescent lighting, I could see peppers of gray in his dark hair. "The mayor is currently reaming the chief and Detective Holden new buttholes. It'll be a minute before she gets to yours."

"I like my butthole right where it is, thank you very much," I told him. "And if I were in the market for a new one, I wouldn't get it from Mayor Green."

Broyles laughed. "You're not afraid of much, are you?"

"I'm afraid of all kinds of things. Just not blowhard politicians who care more about elections than the truth."

He raised his brows. "Were you ever in the military?"

"No, but I grew up the daughter of the chief of police here in Garden Cove. Being his child was kind of like being in the military." I grimaced when I remembered his memory of wretched combat. "Sorry," I apologized. "My upbringing was nothing like what you went through."

He shrugged. "It's no never mind to me. I get it. My dad was an MP in the army. He's the reason I joined. There's a lot of pressure to follow in a parent's footsteps."

"But you became a demolitions expert, not an MP," I pointed out.

He smiled, making his face appear more youthful, and spread his hands. "But look at me now?"

"You're still a demolition guy but also a cop."

"The best of both worlds."

I shook my head at his bravado. It seemed to me that it took a certain kind of person to play with explosives—one that liked to live on the edge and didn't always care about dying.

Reese came into the bullpen. "Hey, Nora," she greeted. "Looking spiffy."

"Then mission accomplished," I told her. "Spiffy was the aim."

"Then bullseye." She mimicked drawing a bow and shooting an arrow. "We just processed Edgar. I've never seen a man cry so much. He went through an entire box of tissue between fingerprinting and mug shots."

"Has he lawyered up?"

"Nope." She gave a low whistle. "For a smart guy, he's kind of dumb."

Poor Edgar. He was going to go to jail—go directly to jail, and not collect two hundred bucks—if he didn't wise up. I was half tempted to call Jasper Riley to take his case. I wouldn't, of course. I was in enough trouble already, apparently.

While waiting for my turn with the angry mayor, I hummed the theme song from "2001: A Space Odyssey."

"I can't believe that movie came out in nineteen sixty-eight," Broyles said. "The man was ahead of his time."

"The theme song was composed by Richard Strauss in eighteen ninety-six." I gave him a "yep, I said eighteen ninety-six" nod. "Strauss was ahead of his time."

"My buddies and I would binge old sci-fi when I was at AIT at Elgin Air Force Base in Florida."

"I thought you were in the Army."

"He was," Reese answered. "He trained as an explosive ordnance specialist at Elgin, though."

"Okay," I said to Broyles. "I gotta ask. Do you think the person doing this has demolition training?"

"What, you don't believe it's the banker?" he asked, sounding doubtful. Then he shook his head. "The materials this guy is using aren't weapon-grade. They're chemicals almost anyone can get hold of. I don't think he's a pro."

"Okay, that's good insight. I didn't think about that. You mentioned something about fuming acid igniting latex. Why is it different?"

"Nitric acid available to the public has a much lower concentration of acid than fuming nitric acid." He took out his phone and showed me a video. A guy sprayed a glove with the acid, and it burst into flames.

"Woah," I said. "That's very cool."

"What's your take on Edgar Jones, Nora?" Reese asked. "You usually have a sixth sense, no psychic pun intended, about these cases."

"I don't think Edgar is our guy. This man... he seems more like a geek or a nerd," Reese commented.

"Edgar is totally a nerd," Reese commented.

"I mean, like a science fiction and science fact kind of nerd."

Reese peered at Broyles. "You mean like Tony?"

"Tony, huh?" She flushed. "That's his name."

"It is," Broyles agreed. There was a hint of amusement in his tone. "Am I a suspect?"

"No," I replied. Not because he wasn't capable. The guy loved movies, science fiction, and he was an expert in stuff that blew up. But when that stink bomb went off, I saw one of the worst days, I assumed, of his life. If he'd been responsible for what was going on, he wouldn't have picked something so triggering.

"That's it?" he asked jovially, "just 'no'?"

"If you had been the guy, I would have seen it already. You have some very strong emotions."

He paled, then nodded. "Gotcha."

"Well, I, for one, am comforted that you have gotten Nora's seal of approval," Reese said.

"I wouldn't go that far," I snickered.

Broyles laughed again. "I'm sorry for the way I treated you before."

"It's fine," I told him. "My ability can be hard for people to believe. I struggled with it myself. Besides, we live in Missouri. Sometimes you've got to show to know."

He chuckled. "You showed me."

"I sure did." I glanced down the corridor that led to Shawn's office. "At this rate, I think she's knitting them a butthole necklace."

"What?" Reese asked, confused.

Broyles gave her a barely perceptible headshake and said, "I'll explain it later."

"Cripes, what fresh hell am I living in?" a woman behind us asked. I knew the voice immediately. Carol Flipping Billingsly. Whatever I'd done in this life or another, I can't believe it warranted this kind of payback.

I crossed my arms over my chest. "What are you doing here, Carol?"

"I could ask you the same," she countered.

"I was summoned."

"Hah!" She smiled smugly. "I was invited."

"Potatoes, po-tah-toes."

"The mayor is going to give me an exclusive," she bragged. "Edgar Jones, Prank Bank Mastermind."

I almost choked on my own spit. "That headline is heinous."

"You're heinous," Carol said. "I can't wait to expose all your secrets, Nora. Then people will know what I've known all along. You're a selfish, entitled brat."

"In what past life did I hurt you?" Holy cow, the woman really had it in for me. "Is this about Shawn?"

She screwed into a sideways pucker. "Shawn?"

"Rafferty," I said. "You know, the chief of police and my ex-husband. Is this because you had a crush on him in high school?"

Carol's laugh was almost maniacal.

Broyles muttered, "Nora was married to the chief?"

Reese shushed him. "Unless it gets physical, we're staying out of it."

"You're kidding, right?" Carol shook her head in disbelief. "You don't even know what you did, do you, Nora?" She put a lot of ugly emphasis on my name as if it were a cuss word.

I returned the favor. "I think we've established that, Carol."

"I worked hard to get recommendations to go to Girls' State our junior year, but they chose you to go instead."

"I didn't even go to Girls' State," I said, full of confusion. Girls' State was a week-long summer leadership program awarded to one or two high school juniors from each school in Missouri every year. You couldn't apply to the program; you had to be nominated by your teachers as a leader. I had no interest in politics or public office. Girls' State would've been wasted on me.

"Exactly! It could've opened so many doors for me, but they gave the opportunity to a rich, entitled daddy's girl who didn't even want it!" Spittle was flying off her lips. "You know you only got in because your dad was the chief."

"Oh my gosh, Carol. Get over it. I am sorry you didn't get into Girls' State. It's not my fault. I was sixteen years old and had no control over who they chose or why. The only thing I could control was if I wanted to go, and I didn't. I didn't do that to spite you. I did it because I was sixteen and wanted to spend the summer with my boyfriend, who had just graduated from high school and was heading off to college." I was pretty sure I was spitting now. I took a deep breath to calm myself. "I'm sorry your life didn't work out the way you expected. I think anyone past the age of forty can attest to the fact that it rarely does. You're old enough now to know better than to blame a hormonal teen for the decisions she made in the past." Besides, it wasn't like the program would've taken Carol had I not been nominated. After all, there were two positions available, and she hadn't been offered either one.

My reasoning seemed to take the wind out of her sails, but it didn't stop her from glaring at me. Well, at least now I knew. Carol Billingsly still had the emotional maturity of a sixteen-year-old, and if she hadn't grown out of it by now, she probably never would.

Ezra walked up the hall, shaking his head as he entered the room.

"Do we still have jobs, Boss?" Reese asked.

"Yep," he said. His gaze found mine, and his eyes softened around the edges. "No one is losing their job. No one."

I exhaled my relief. "Then why have I been called in?"

He stared at Carol. "We found out that the anony-mous letters were written by Carol Billingsly. She tried to cover her trail, but the owner of the paper gave us backdoor access to her work computer, and her keystrokes were logged last night at a quarter after ten. She's our concerned citizen."

"So," Carol huffed. "I didn't do anything illegal. I spoke the truth. Nora is a menace to this town."

"I'm mighty certain the only menace here is you," Reese said in my defense.

"The chief and the mayor are talking with Darla Potter, the owner of the Gazette, and she is planning to issue a public apology for any wrongdoing on behalf of her staff."

Carol's skin turned sallow. "She... she can't do that."

"What you wrote about Ms. Black and then tried to pass off as an anonymous letter is a libel," Ezra continued. "That's beyond ethical journalism, and our prosecutor thinks we have a strong case if Ms. Black wants to move forward with it."

"I guess I'll have to think on it," I replied.

Carol blanched.

I had no intention of suing the wretched woman, but she didn't need to know that. The words she'd written about me were so vile that I didn't think I could forgive her, but I wasn't interested in taking her to court over it. The trial would only expose me and my gift even more.

"Good ol' Nora." Carol's eyes were glassy. She spoke in a barely audible whisper, and I had to lean in to make out the words. "Always the hero. We'll see how much after tonight."

I narrowed my gaze at the reporter. "What do you mean by that?"

"You'll see," she hissed. "This race isn't over. Watch yourself, baby, or you'll get burned."

"Light up the sky like the fourth of July," the mystery man had said in the memory, "I'm coming in hot, dog, and the race is on. Wow, wow. Try an' stop me. I'm unstoppable. Stop, drop, and roll, hero, or let it burn, baby, burn."

Was it a coincidence that Carol had used some of those words? I didn't think so. I turned to Ezra. "She's part of this," I told him.

"Part of what?"

"Carol is in league with The Scent Stalker."

She glowered at me. "Prove it."

"Not a denial." Ezra rested his hand on his holster. "That's good enough for me."

"She said there's something coming tonight," I told him. "If we can't stop it, someone's going to burn."

"You'll burn, they'll burn, everyone will burn," Carol seethed as Reese put her in handcuffs. "You'll all burn in hell."

My stomach lurched as the implication settled in. Carol was in cahoots with the man tormenting me. Had she been in league with him this whole time? Whatever the case was, I couldn't shake the awful feeling that tonight was the big finale of their plan.

"We have to find her partner," I told them. "We have to find him and stop him."

"So..." Broyles scratched his jaw. "Does this mean Jones isn't the guy?"

"Jones is not the guy," Ezra confirmed. "How long do you think we have?"

"Light up the sky like the fourth of July," I told him. "I think as soon as it's dark, all bets are off. We have about four hours to figure it out." How many people would suffer if we couldn't? As far as I was concerned, even one would be too many.

SEVENTEEN

"No, no, no," Allison Green whined. "This is over. Finished. We caught the bad guy. The people cheered."

"Edgar is not the bad guy," I insisted for the fifth time. "Did he know how his coin ended up in the alley behind the florist?"

"He says it isn't his coin," Shawn replied, "but his fingerprints were on it, plain and simple."

I shot my ex-husband a sour look. "Why are you so determined to pin this on Edgar?"

"I'm not," he protested. "I'm just following the evidence."

"Sorry, chief, but I'm with Nora on this," Ezra interjected.

"Big surprise," Shawn muttered. He sighed heavily. "Go ahead. Tell me why she's right."

Oh God, it was starting to feel like when we were

married. He would get bent out of shape when I was right, and he was wrong. We didn't have time for this absurd banter.

Ezra respectfully said, "We've gone through his house, his garage, his car, and his office. We haven't found a single other piece of evidence linking him to the crimes."

"Then why did he run?" Allison demanded. "Innocent people don't run."

"That's a myth," Shawn told her. He was starting to act like a reasonable man. "Lots of innocent people run just like the guilty ones. Sometimes people are just scared."

"In two days, Edgar was injured in a blast and almost got gassed at an AA meeting. I think we can all understand why he might've been scared," I added.

The mayor huffed. "Fine, but if Edgar isn't the guy, are we sure Carol was alone in this? Maybe she's the Scented Stalker."

Ezra cringed at the name. "Nora said she heard a male voice."

"Through a mask," Green shot back, losing her already dissipating cool. "It could've been staged just like the rest of the visions."

I wanted to fault her logic, but her reasoning was sound. "That doesn't mean she hasn't already set the trap," I said. "She set up the memories ahead of time. There's nothing to say she didn't set the traps up ahead of time as well."

The mayor let out a frustrated growl. "I just got the town back on my side."

"And if napalm hits them tonight, you'll lose them all over again," Ezra reminded her.

"Fine," she snapped. She waved her hand at my face. "You guys investigate Carol, and Nora can do her thing. Just solve this matter quickly and quietly. No muss. No fuss."

I arched my brow at Shawn. He shook his head. I guessed Allison Green was the chief tonight. Oh well, she wasn't saying anything Shawn wouldn't.

"I'll call Judge Watson and have him sign a warrant," Shawn said. "The sooner we can search Carol's place, the sooner we might know what the hell is happening." He clapped his hands. "Four hours until dark, people. Chop chop." As we were leaving his office, I heard him say, "Mayor Green, this is my command. While I serve at your pleasure, I don't run my police force at your pleasure. If you don't like the job I'm doing, fire me. Otherwise, I'll be the one running my officers the way I see fit. Are we clear?"

I half expected the mayor to argue. Instead, she said, "Clear. It won't happen again, Chief Rafferty."

Good for Shawn. I was glad he stood up for himself. He wouldn't have been an effective chief if he hadn't.

Out in the bullpen, Broyles was on the phone, and Reese was at her desk reading some kind of flyer.

"Hey." She waved it at me. "The raft race starts at five. In those homemade pieces of junk, it will take several hours for most of the contestants to go three miles to the dam and back. A lot of them won't finish."

"Okay." I was sure there was a point. "And?"

"They're set to shoot fireworks off at five after nine when the King or Queen of the Lake is crowned." She shrugged. "The sky will be lit up like the Fourth of July."

"The race is on could be a reference to the raft race." Although I'd seen paint dry faster than these handmade floats could move.

"Wait, what? It can't be the raft race," Ezra said, alarm in his voice. "Mason and Ari are competing. They've been working on their float at my cabin all week."

"We have to get them off the water," I told Ezra, though I wasn't sure why. If the bad stuff wasn't going to happen until the fireworks went off, they'd be safe, right? "It's not logical, but I can't focus if I'm worried about them." I needed to know the people I loved were safe. "Gilly," I said. "She and Scott are probably there. I'll text her and see."

I tapped an SOS into the text box and sent it. That was our never-ignore code. Even if she was in the throes of passion, she would immediately text me back. That was the definition of never-ignore.

"We have to figure out who Carol's accomplice is." Ezra's voice was strained. "If we find him, we can stop him, and then everyone will be safe."

I nodded. "Yes, yes. That's what we need to do."

"Got the warrant," Broyles said. He gave Ezra a

studied look. "I can take Nora to the Billingsly house to do her thing if you and Reese want to go to the lake and find your kid."

I nodded to Ezra. "I'll call the minute I see anything that can help."

"And if I get any non-mystical clues, I'll call," Broyles said.

"Okay," Ezra agreed, his voice tight with strain. "I don't like splitting up, but I agree it's best for now."

I walked over to him and wrapped my arms around his waist. He embraced me back. "We'll find the Scent Stalker, and the kids will be safe. Everyone will be safe." I hoped my words were a promise from the universe and not pie-in-the-sky wishful thinking.

CAROL BILLINGSLY's front door creaked open like a spooky invitation. The colonial ranch-style home she lived in had an air of neglected elegance, the original molding on the walls hinted at its former glory. Carol was behind bars, thankfully, but her final words echoed in my mind. *You'll burn, they'll burn, everyone will burn. You'll all burn in hell.*

We had to find her partner before it was too late. Broyles handed me booties for my shoes and evidence bags before handing me a pair of gloves. He shook his head as I slipped the booties over my Gucci shoes. "This has to be the fanciest outfit I've ever seen any cop wear during a search."

"Not a cop," I said, then easily put the large-sized gloves on.

He chuckled. "I guess not. Don't touch anything that looks wet," he cautioned. "Let me check it first to make sure it won't eat through your gloves."

"I'll happily be guided by you," I assured him. I remembered Levi's blistered palms from the nitric acid. I didn't want any of that.

Broyles took the lead as we made our way through the house. I took a deep breath, letting the mingled scents of old wood, coffee, and a faint hint of lavender fill my senses. The living room had a contrasting mix of history and modernity. The furniture was sleek and contemporary, a stark difference to the intricate, time-worn moldings that framed the room. I ran my fingers along the smooth leather of the sofa.

The coffee table was cluttered with copies of the Garden Cove Gazette. Their headlines were stories of political scandals and community events. Carol's work, her life, sprawled out in ink and paper. I picked up the top issue, the one that carried the anonymous letter she'd written about me. The sharp smell of fresh print mixed with the room's mustiness. I got a vision of Carol, giddy, as she read the letter out loud as if it were her victory speech.

Holy cow, Carol seriously hated me. And now that I knew why, I felt pity for the woman who never grew up or learned to take responsibility for her own choices. I was sure she'd spent her whole life lamenting all the bad things that happened to her, all the while never taking steps to make good things happen. What a pathetic waste. However, she'd now crossed a line and was going to have to pay.

"The house is clear," Broyles informed me. "You getting anything, yet?"

"Nothing helpful," I confessed. "I'll keep trying."

"I did a quick search of the kitchen," he said. "Regular household stuff. I'm going to check out the garage than the basement." He pointed to a door off the living room. "Those are the two most likely places after the kitchen for people to store chemicals."

I rolled my hand at him. "If you find any holler. I might be able to get something from the odor."

"You got it, Ms. Black." He winked. "If it stinks, you'll be the first to know."

"You can call me, Nora," I told him. "We're good now, right?"

He grinned. "Yeah, we're good. Call me, Tony."

Excellent. I'd won over the hardnose cop who'd been making my life a little more difficult of late. It made me happy because I actually liked and admired the man. I was putting a check in the win column. I needed all the wins I could get.

I made my way to the kitchen. The scent of lavender was stronger here, probably from the cleaning products under the sink. The countertops were pristine, not a single dish out of place. Carol's meticulous nature was evident, but there was a sense of emptiness as if her home was missing its heart. I opened the fridge. She barely had the basics: milk, eggs, cheese, and a half-eaten sandwich. No clues here.

Heading down the narrow hallway, I noticed a slight scuff on the wooden floor. I crouched down, touching the mark. It was recent, maybe from a hurried step or a dragged piece of furniture. I followed the trail to a small study. The air here was different, charged with a subtle energy. The desk was a modern glass affair, papers neatly stacked, a laptop closed and locked.

Bookshelves lined the walls, filled with a mix of classic literature and contemporary thrillers. One book, thicker and dustier than the others, caught my eye. I pulled it out, the cover stiff and unyielding. Inside, instead of pages, there was a hollow space containing a small, black notebook. My heart quickened.

The notebook was filled with Carol's cramped hand-writing, detailing meetings, interviews, and something more cryptic: dates and locations, including the Cove Community Church. I didn't know what the significance was, but I bagged the notebook for forensics.

I realized that Gilly hadn't called or texted me back. My never-ignore was being ignored, and it worried me.

"Anything?" I yelled at Broyles.

"No sulfur or nitric acid," he bellowed back. "But there is something you should come see in the garage."

When I joined him, I was shocked by what I saw. The

walls and floor had been painted white, and dead leaves and stems were swept into a corner. Several blushes of pink marked where Starfighter lilies had been smashed against the ground.

"This is it," I told him. "This is where I had the vision when the lilies were delivered. I don't know if it was her or her partner, but this is where the stink bomb was made."

I suspected it was her partner. Her house was spotless. If she'd been the one to clean up the garage after the floral arranging, she would've done the job right.

"Basement?" Broyles asked.

I nodded. "Yep. And I'd bet we find a popcorn maker and a box of bullets."

The basement steps were steep, but I managed the descent without too much trouble, thanks to the injections I received in my knees every six months. I was right about the popcorn stand, wrong about the bullets.

"This is definitely the basement from my first vision." I sniffed the air, detecting an odor I couldn't identify. "Is that gas?"

Broyles inhaled and said, "It's kerosene."

"Is there any stored down here?" I walked around the area, trying to find where the odor was stronger.

The basement is cold and gray. The air is thick with the acrid scent of kerosene, making it hard to breathe. In my visions, I don't see faces. They're always blurry, but there are two people in the room—a man and a woman. The woman's shape and hair make her easily recognizable. It's Carol.

They're whisper-arguing in the corner. The man is wearing a hoodie, and I can see his hair or what his size might be, but next to Carol, he seems...small. On top of that, his voice strikes a chord of familiarity. Carol's words cut through clear and sharp.

"I'll pay you the five hundred dollars, okay? Just give me some time," she snaps, her tone edged with frustration. "I just dropped a thousand for that flower delivery."

"This was your plan, not mine. I didn't use my own supplies for free. I'm here for the money." The man isn't backing down. "You owe me for the stink bomb, Carol. Five hundred dollars. I need the money. No more excuses."

The tension in the room is palpable. A clang-clang resounds through the space, sending a shiver down my spine. I recognize the clock from a previous vision.

"I hate that clock," Carol mutters, her voice dripping with disdain.

The man's response is quick and defensive. "It's a family antique. I need you to keep it safe for a couple of days."

She scoffs, crossing her arms. "It's noisy and irritating." She waves off his protest and opens the door to a storage area under the stairs. There are several large canisters of kerosene, at least fifteen gallons each, clearly marked with warning labels. Sounding pleased, she says, "This is what you'll need for our main event."

"Oh, boy," I said as the vision faded, and a sudden realization hit me.

I looked at Broyles. "I know who's been helping her."

I walked over to the antique clock on the floor behind a pillar. I picked it up and saw a plate inside the face.

"What are you looking at?" Broyles asked.

I showed him the nameplate.

"Daniel Lems." He looked confused.

"That's the man who owns the antique furniture shop next to my boutique."

He furrowed his brow. "And you think he's Carol's partner?"

"Not him," I replied. "It's his son. It's Waylon Lems."

EIGHTEEN

E zra hadn't answered his phone when I called, so Broyles used the police radio to get a hold of Reese.

Reese's voice came over the air. "Cell phone reception is crap here," she complained. "I hope you all found something because we're coming up empty here. Over."

"Request a secure channel," I told Broyles. I wanted to ask about Ari and Mason, and to see if Reese had seen Gilly, and I didn't want to broadcast it out to all the cops in the area."

"Move to two. Over," Broyles said. He reached down and turned the dial on his radio until the LED number read 2. "Done."

"Thanks." I held out my hand, and he handed me the radio.

"Suspect first," he advised.

"Right." I depressed the button on the side of the

handheld. "Suspect is Waylon Lems, white male, early forties, five-eight, around one hundred and thirty pounds. His hair is light brown, shoulder-length. He is possibly transporting several fifteen-gallon barrels of kerosene for whatever he has planned. Over." I took my hand off the button.

"One hundred and fifty? Did I hear that correctly? Over." Her voice hardened. She sounded every bit a cop.

"Yes. Motive, other than money, unknown. Over." Some psychopaths got their kicks on torturing people. Maybe that was all the motive Waylon needed. "Have you seen Gilly? The kids? Over."

"Gilly, the Doc, and Ezra took a jon boat with a trolling motor out on the lake to track them down. It's going to be tough. The kids are somewhere among the hundreds of entries this year. There's one raft that's ten feet high and made out of nothing but Styrofoam coolers. These people are nuts. Over."

"Heard. Over." I was relieved she'd found Gilly and let her know something was up, but now I was worried for the three of them out searching for the kids.

I handed the radio back to Broyles. "We're coming in now," he said. "Over. Where do you want us to meet you?"

"The marina," Reese answered. "Over."

*****

We pulled into Portman's on the Lake marina parking lot to a scene of chaos. The homemade raft race had drawn a massive crowd of spectators—drunk tourists, sunburned families, and locals alike—all eagerly watching the ludicrous floats bobbing on the water. Broyles and I scanned the throng, looking for Reese among the sea of faces.

Broyles keyed his radio, trying to establish contact. "Reese, this is Broyles. We're at the marina. Over."

Static crackled before Reese's voice responded, sounding frustrated. "Copy that. En route to dock six. Meet me there. Over."

"Copy that. Over." Broyles tucked the radio away. "Let's move," he said, urgency coloring his voice as we hurried through the lively crowd toward the marina. It was after seven now, but it was still hot as we navigated through the maze of excited spectators. It almost made me long for winter. Almost.

As we reached the marina's edge to wait for Reese, I scanned the horizon, hoping to catch sight of Ezra and the others. The sound of raucous cheers and the splashing of water filled the air, but amidst the festivities, our mission to find Waylon weighed heavily on my mind. I couldn't shake the feeling there was more to his participation than for money or the fun of it. Waylon had always been so nice—*said every neighbor of a serial killer.* Waylon's dad, however, was a piece of work. He was verbally, and I think, at times, physically abusive to his son. Even now. I always thought Waylon's sculptures were an outlet—an escape—from his dad. If someone had told me Mr. Lems had people tied up in the basement, I wouldn't have blinked. Which is why I wanted to understand.

"Hey, guys," Reese said as she hustled toward us. She looked at my feet. "Nora, you picked the wrong day for a Gucci."

"You're telling me." If I'd had time to go home and change clothes, I would've. Instead, the only thing I could do was take the blazer off. "Have you heard from Ezra?"

"You mean in the last five minutes since you asked?" She smiled. "Yes, he's fine. They found Ari and Mason. They're escorting them back."

"Poor kids. They were really looking forward to this, then Waylon and Carol had to spoil it."

"Every party needs a pooper," Reese said. "The water patrol has been alerted so we can get the rest of the poor bastards off the water. Got uniforms searching the cars, the crowd, and the bank along the lake. If Waylon's here, we'll find him."

I liked her optimism, but this place was packed. Needle meet haystack. "What about me?" I asked. "Should I join the search?"

"Not in those shoes," Reese said. "Besides, Ezra said to wait for him here at dock six. He's on his way back now, so hopefully, it won't be too long. Broyles and I will join the search."

Broyles took his radio off, twisted the dial to change the channel back to regular and handed it to me. "Just in case."

"Thanks," I said gratefully. Twenty minutes later, I was still standing in the same spot, my feet sore and my shoulders getting sunburned. I used the radio. "Ezra, where are you at?"

"Drunken idiots capsized their raft. Mounting a rescue. Over."

Great. I couldn't be mad because he was helping people, right? I was more mad at myself for my style than for my comfort.

"Miss," a woman said. "Where's the nearest bathroom?"

I shook my head. "Do I look like I work here?"

She shrugged. "Kinda."

Six more people asked me for directions to the bar, what time the fireworks started, and where they could get more towels. My bad for wearing a suit to a resort in the middle of summer. Come on, Ezra, I thought. Hurry up.

I scanned the incoming boats. Nothing yet. At some point, I was dazing as I watched a white pickup back down into the woods using a service road entrance at the end of the docks. While the mules were more comfortable than regular heels, they weren't tennis shoes. After another thirty minutes of being wedged in, my toes were starting to cramp.

A young woman wearing water shoes passed me on the dock. "What size shoe do you wear?" I asked.

"An eight," she replied.

I was a seven and a half, so close enough. "Can I buy them from you?"

"I'll trade you for yours," she said slyly.

"Uh, no," I told her. "How about fifty bucks?"

"Sold!" she said, already sliding out of them.

I got two twenties and a ten from my purse, then took off my mules and tucked them inside. Thankfully, the water shoes hadn't been in the water yet, so they were dry.

I got on the radio again. "ETA to dock?"

"Another fifteen minutes," Ezra answered.

I slapped a mosquito away, twisting as it buzzed my cheek. That's when I noticed the service vehicle at the edge of the lake, with a man crouching near the water. I pulled out my phone and activated the camera, zooming in. My breath caught. The image was a little blurry, but I was almost certain I'd found Waylon.

Grabbing the radio from my purse, I pressed the button. "Suspect located," I said urgently. "I repeat, suspect located."

No one answered. I checked the radio to make sure it was working. It squawked so the batteries were good. Then I noticed the channel had changed.

I switched it to two. "Reese. Broyles. I see Waylon." Still no answer.

What had Broyles changed the channel to before he'd left?

Even from this distance, I could see three white

barrels turned on their sides. I got out my phone again and zoomed in.

What the heck? Was he dumping kerosene into the lake?

I moved the phone to view the incoming boats. They were going to cross right past Waylon's dump site. Ezra had said he was on his way back. A sick feeling churned in my stomach—Waylon was planning to ignite the kerosene when the boats passed by.

Burn, baby, burn.

My stomach clenched with fury. I couldn't let that happen. I had to stop him before he could carry out his plan. I cursed myself for not carrying my gun in my purse. I had a concealed carry license, but I didn't like having my weapon with me all the time, especially since JP had started getting her toddler hands into everything. That didn't mean I was defenseless, though. I had pepper spray and a telescoping flashlight in my purse.

I jogged around the dock to the parking lot, following the asphalt to where I'd seen the truck enter the service road. It was a longer route, but it was faster than climbing over the rocks at the shore. I switched numbers on the radio one by one, asking for anyone to answer as I neared Waylon's location.

Finally, when I got to sixteen, Ezra answered. "Where are you?"

"Suspect located," I said frantically. "He's down a service road on the right side of the docks. He's parked a truck and is dumping kerosene into the lake. I repeat, dumping forty-five gallons of kerosene. I think he plans to light it up when the boats cross over."

"Nora, hold your position," Ezra said. "Help is on the way. Do not approach the suspect."

"He's going to light people on fire," I called back, panic rising. I was close enough now to see Waylon had a box of Roman candles on the hood of his truck. Clever. He could use those to shoot fireballs onto the spreading fuel. Maybe I wouldn't have to confront Waylon if I could find a way to steal his igniter. He was preoccupied with dumping the kerosene, and if I was lucky, I could get away with it before he noticed.

I turned the volume off on the radio so it wouldn't give my location away as I quietly crept toward the truck, using the trees for cover as much as possible.

A slew of rafts was returning, getting closer to Waylon's trap. I quickened my steps, my heart pounding like a jackhammer in my chest.

Just as I reached the candles, he turned around. *Fuuuudge.*

"Waylon!" Ezra's authoritative and firm voice cut through the silence. He was in the jon boat by himself, so he must've passed Gilly and Scott off to another boat or raft, then used the motor to come straight to me. Unfortunately, he was floating on a sea of flammable fuel. "Stop right there."

Oh, God. He was going to get fried.

Waylon spun around, eyes wide with surprise and then fury. He was holding an old-fashioned Zippo lighter in his hand, and he'd struck the flame. "Stay back," he snarled, his voice cracking with the weight of his mania. "Or I'll light you up."

"Stop this, Waylon," I begged, stepping forward, my hands raised in a placating gesture. "You don't want to do this. Think about the people, the families'…"

For a split second, he hesitated, his eyes flickering with something almost human. But then he shook his head, a wild gleam returning. "I…I don't…It's too late," he said. He took a step toward me. "Stay back!"

"Waylon!" Ezra shouted, and the man whipped around, his back to me once again. My fear for Ezra made me reckless. I reached into my bag and grabbed the easiest weapon at hand then charged the last twenty feet with my telescoping flashlight extended, lunged forward, and knocked the lighter from Waylon's hand before tackling him to the ground. The lighter skittered down the boat ramp toward the water when we hit the rough cement. I held my breath as I waited for the water to ignite.

Nothing happened. "The flames out," Ezra shouted.

I heard him splash in the water as the strong scent of kerosene overpowered my senses. No, no, I thought. Not now.

The vision didn't care that I was about to get my butt whooped.

I'm in an old, cluttered antique furniture shop. I recognize it immediately as Mr. Lems place. The smell of kerosene is suffocating. There's a man on the floor, bleeding from his head, and it's not hard to tell by his sheer size that it's Waylon's father.

"You won't get away with this," Mr. Lems says. I can see he's been tied with some twine to a ring on the floor.

"You're wrong," Waylon tells him. It's an old shop, and you have a whole section with kerosene lanterns. The fire investigators won't blink an eye. He has a timer in his hand, similar to the one he put on the stink bomb. "At five after nine, while the whole town is watching the fire at the lake, you'll be enjoying your own personal inferno. By the time the firetrucks get here, it'll be too late.

"Why, son?"

"Because I'm tired. I can't do this anymore. This is the only way I'll be free of you."

The vision snapped away, leaving me gasping for breath. I turned to see Ezra, soaking wet, yanking Waylon off me and pinning him to the ground. He pressed his knee into Waylon's back. "Nora, you all right?" he asked, his voice strained but steady.

"Yeah." My elbows were scrapped up, and I rubbed the back of my neck. As much as it hurt, I knew it would be worse in the morning. "I'm okay."

"Nice shoes," he teased, then whistled low, a tight smile on his lips. "Damn, woman, you're going to age me twenty years."

I chuckled. "Then I'll have to trade you in on a new model." I picked up a foot and wiggled it. "And these shoes are the most expensive water shoes on the lake." I sobered as the reality of the vision hit me. "We've got to get fire trucks over to Lems Antique Furniture. Waylon dumped kerosene around Mr. Lems and set a timer to start a fire in the store. He's trying to kill his father. That's what this has been about."

Not money. Not revenge. Just a man who was still an angry child at heart, who couldn't find a way to grow up and leave his father. Not while his father still lived. No wonder Carol and he found each other. They were two peas in an emotionally stunted pod.

"Get a squad car, an ambulance, and fire services over to Lems Furniture," he said into his radio before rattling off the address. "Tell them to be careful. There's flammable liquid set to go on a timer."

"Nine-oh-five," I told him.

He shook his head and smirked. "Five after nine."

Broyles and Reese showed up shortly and cuffed him. When they finished, they wrestled Waylon to his feet. The man's rage had given way to broken sobbing, the fight drained out of him.

"I wonder what it's going to take to clean this up?" I asked.

"More know-how than I got," Ezra replied. His eyes filled with a mix of pride and worry as he met my gaze. "You did good, Nora," he said softly. "We stopped him."

*****

Ezra's cabin was warm and rustic, and tonight, it felt like a sanctuary, a world away from the chaos and danger we'd left behind.

A week had passed since Carol and Waylon had plotted to turn Garden Cove Lake into an inferno. They were both in jail, awaiting arraignment for two counts of reckless endangerment, multiple counts of assault, attempted murder, and arson. They were both looking at a long time inside of a cell. Unsurprisingly, they'd turned on each other and provided even more damning evidence to keep them locked up for a good long time. To me, hatred was a wasted emotion. To them... it had been their modus operandi and had backfired in a way that had destroyed them.

Waylon admitted to stealing Edgar Jones' coin from his desk at the bank when he'd gone in with his father the previous month to ask for a loan. He'd had an idea in his head to frame Edgar at the point, and the fact that the poor banker had been on scene at the first two dangerous pranks had been a happy accident. Needless to say, Edgar was released with an apology from the police department. I think that had been the mayor's idea. The last thing the city needed was a wrongful arrest suit, and since Edgar was a prominent citizen in Garden Cove, he'd have a good chance of winning.

The mayor awarded commendations to Shawn, Ezra, and all of Ezra's team for valor in the line of duty. For me, she offered a private, heartfelt thank you and promised my name would not grace any public records. I was extremely grateful. The Garden Cove Gazette issued a front-page apology, blaming the letter on the crazy ravings of a madwoman with a vendetta going all the way back to high school. With Carol in jail, it helped to sell the story as completely believable. I'd been getting less hate now, and maybe in a short while, folks would forget about it altogether. I doubted that would happen, but a girl could hope.

The fire department got to Mr. Lems in time. They saved the old coot's life. He hadn't been grumpy but grateful. Lucky for me, he'd decided to finally sell the building, and he offered me a fair price. I needed the extra storage for my stock, and it would give Gilly the space to expand her massage business. Ari and Mason did not finish the race, but neither did anyone. The state water patrol had evacuated everyone else in the area off the lake. As it was, Portman's docks were shut down until the EPA could contain, clean, and decontaminate the affected water.

"Are you okay?" Ezra asked as I nestled into his side, feeling the steady beat of his heart against my cheek. His arm was wrapped around me, holding me close, a silent promise of protection and love.

"I'm perfect," I told him. "You?"

"I think you're perfect, too." He grinned.

I gave his chest a playful slap. "That's not what I meant."

"I know," he said, stroking the hair from my face. "I'm about as good as a man can get."

Across the room, Ezra's son Mason and my goddaughter Ari sat on the floor, their eyes wide with fascination as they watched "2001: A Space Odyssey" for the first time. The movie's eerie score and stunning visuals filled the room, but I was more captivated by the peaceful scene around me. The two twenty-year-olds were engrossed in the film, their friendship evident in their easy banter and shared wonder.

Ezra chuckled softly, his breath warm against my hair. "I think they're hooked," he whispered, his voice filled with affection.

I smiled, snuggling closer. "It's a classic. Hard not to be."

We fell into a comfortable silence, the weight of recent events lifting as we soaked in the simple joy of being together. I glanced over at Mason and Ari, their faces lit by the flickering light of the TV screen and felt a swell of gratitude. They were safe, here with us, their laughter and curiosity a balm to my weary soul.

Ezra's fingers traced lazy patterns on my arm, a soothing rhythm that lulled me into a state of contentment. "I'm glad you're here," he murmured, his voice a low rumble that resonated deep within me.

"Me too," I replied, tilting my head to look up at him. His eyes, filled with warmth and love, met mine. "We did good, Ezra. The bad guys are put away, and the people we care about are safe."

He nodded, his lips moving over mine. "All is right with the world." His smile was a soft curve that made my heart flutter.

"Indeed," I agreed. "It's never been more right."

The End...for now.

What's next for Nora and the gang?

Of Spice and Men: A Nora Black Midlife Psychic Mystery Book 10

My name is Nora Black. I'm fifty-six years old, and I'm having the midlife adventure of my life.

I'm all set for the ultimate escape: a couples cruise with my sweetheart Ezra, and my best friends Gilly and Pippa, along with their husbands.

We are ready to hit the high seas for sun, fun, and definitely no crime-solving. The plan is simple: cocktails, sunsets, and endless laughter. But you know what they say about the best-laid plans...

When one of our table mates, a frequent flyer on this very cruise line, ends up face down in the Lido Deck pool, the captain declares it an accident.

But my psychic nose says otherwise—this is murder. Now, with the clock ticking before we reach foreign soil, I'll have to use my aroma mojo to sniff out the truth. It looks like it's up to us to unravel the mystery before the killer gets away with murder.

So much for smooth sailing!

PIT PERFECT MURDER

BARKSIDE OF THE MOON COZY MYSTERIES
BOOK 1

Chapter 1 - Sneak Peek

When I was eighteen years old, I came home from a sleepover and found my mom and dad with their throats cut, and their hearts ripped from their chests.

My little brother Danny was in a broom closet in the kitchen, his arms wrapped around his knees, and his face pale and ghostly. Until that day, I'd planned to go to college and study medicine after graduation, but instead, I ended up staying home and taking care of my seven-year-old brother.

Seventeen years later, my brother was murdered. At the time, Danny's death looked like it would go unsolved, much like my parents' had.

Without Haze Kinsey, my best friend since we were five, the killers would have gotten away with it. She was a special agent for the FBI for almost a decade, and when I called her about Danny's death, she dropped everything to come help me get him justice. The evil group of witches and Shifters responsible for the decimation of my family paid with their lives.

Yes. I said witches and Shifters. Did I forget to mention I'm a werecougar? Oh, and my friend Hazel is a witch. Recently, I discovered witches in my own family tree on my mother's side. Shifters, in general, only mated with Shifters, but witches were the exception. As a matter of fact, my friend Haze is mated to a bear Shifter.

I wouldn't have known about the witch in my genealogy, though, if a rogue witch coven hadn't done some funky hoodoo witchery to me. Apparently, the spell activated a latent talent that had been dormant in my hybrid genes.

My ancestor's magic acted like truth serum to anyone who came near her. No one could lie in her presence. Lucky me, my ability was a much lesser form of hers. People didn't have to tell me the truth, but whenever they were around me, they had the compulsion to overshare all sorts of private matters about themselves. This can get seriously uncomfortable for all parties involved. Like, the fact that I didn't need to know that Janet Strickland had been wearing the same pair of underwear for an entire week, or that Mike Dandridge had sexual fantasies about clowns.

My newfound talent made me unpopular and unwelcome in a town full of paranormal creatures who thrived on little deceptions. So, when Haze discovered the whereabouts of my dad's brother, a guy I hadn't known even existed, I sold all my belongings, let the bank have my parents' house, jumped in my truck, and headed south.

After two days and 700 miles of nonstop gray, snowy weather, I pulled my screeching green and yellow mini-truck into an auto repair shop called The Rusty Wrench. Much like my beloved pickup, I'd needed a new start, and moving to a small town occupied by humans seemed the best shot. I'd barely made it to Moonrise, Missouri before my truck began its death throes. The vehicle protested the last 127 miles by sputtering to a halt as I rolled her into the closest spot.

The shop was a small white-brick building with a one-car garage off to the right side. A black SUV and a white compact car occupied two of the six parking spots.

A sign on the office door said: *No Credit Cards. Cash Only. Some Local Checks Accepted (Except from Earl—You Know Why, Earl! You check-bouncing bastard).*

A man in stained coveralls, wiping a greasy tool with a rag, came out the side door of the garage. He had a full head of wavy gray hair, bushy eyebrows over light blue, almost colorless eyes, and a minimally lined face that made me wonder about his age. I got out of the truck to greet him.

"Can I help you, miss?" His voice was soft and raspy with a strong accent that was not quite Deep South.

"Yes, please." I adjusted my puffy winter coat. "The

heater stopped working first. Then the truck started jerking for the last fifty miles or so."

He scratched his stubbly chin. "You could have thrown a rod, sheared the distributor, or you have a bad ignition module. That's pretty common on these trucks."

I blinked at him. I could name every muscle in the human body and twelve different kinds of viruses, but I didn't know a spark plug from a radiator cap. "And that all means..."

"If you threw a rod, the engine is toast. You'll need a new vehicle."

"Crap." I grimaced. "What if it's the other thingies?"

The scruffy mechanic shrugged. "A sheared distributor is an easy fix, but I have to order in the part, which means it won't get fixed for a couple of days. Best-case scenario, it's the ignition module. I have a few on hand. Could get you going in a couple of hours, but..." he looked over my shoulder at the truck and shook his head, "...I wouldn't get your hopes up."

I must've looked really forlorn because the guy said, "It might not need any parts. Let me take a look at it first. You can grab a cup of coffee across the street at Langdon's One-Stop."

He pointed to the gas station across the road. It didn't look like much. The pale-blue paint on the front of the building looked in need of a new coat, and the weather-beaten sign with the store's name on it had seen better days. There was a car at the gas pumps and a couple more in the parking lot, but not enough to call it busy.

I'd had enough of one-stops, though, thank you. The bathrooms had been horrible enough to make a wereraccoon yark, and it took a lot to make those garbage eaters sick. Besides, I wasn't just passing through Moonrise, Missouri.

"Have you ever heard of The Cat's Meow Café?" Saying the name out loud made me smile the way it had when Hazel had first said it to me. I'd followed my GPS into town, so I knew I wasn't too far away from the place.

"Just up the street about two blocks, take a right on Sterling Street. You can't miss it. I should have some news in about an hour or so, but take your time."

"Thank you, Mister..."

"Greer." He shoved the tool in his pocket. "Greer Knowles."

"I'm Lily Mason."

"Nice to meet ya," said Greer. "The place gets hoppin' around noon. That's when church lets out."

I looked at my phone. It was a little before noon now. "Good. I could go for something to eat. How are the burgers?"

"Best in town," he quipped.

I laughed. "Good enough."

Even in the sub-freezing temperature, my hands were sweating in my mittens. I wasn't sure what had me more nervous, leaving the town I grew up in for the first time in my life or meeting an uncle I'd never known existed.

I crossed a four-way intersection. One of the signs was missing, and I saw the four-by-four post had snapped off at its base. I hadn't noticed it on my way in. Crap. Had I run a stop sign? I walked the two blocks to Sterling. The diner was just where Greer had said. A blue truck, a green mini-coup, and a sheriff's SUV were parked out front.

An alarm dinged as the glass door opened to The Cat's Meow. Inside, there was a row of six booths along the wall, four tables that seated four out in the open floor, and counter seating with about eight cushioned black stools. The interior décor was rustic country with orange tabby kitsch everywhere. A man in blue jeans and a button-down shirt with a string tie sat in the nearest booth. A female police officer sat at a counter chair sipping coffee and eating a cinnamon roll. Two elderly women, one with snowball-white hair, the other a dyed strawberry-blonde, sat in a back booth.

The white poof-headed lady said, "This egg is not over-medium."

"Well, call the mayor," said Redhead. "You're unhappy with your eggs. Again."

"See this?" She pointed at the offending egg. "Slime, right here. Egg snot. You want to eat it?"

"If it'll make you shut up about breakfast food, I'll eat it and lick the plate."

A man with copper-colored hair and a thick beard,

tall and well-muscled, stepped out of the kitchen. He wore a white apron around his waist, and he had on a black T-shirt and blue jeans. He held a plate with a single fried egg shining in the middle.

The old woman with the snowy hair blushed, her thin skin pinking up as he crossed the room to their table. "Here you go, Opal. Sorry 'bout the mix-up on your egg." He slid the plate in front of her. "This one is pure perfection." He grinned, his broad smile shining. "Just like you." He winked.

Opal giggled.

The redhead rolled her eyes. "You're as easy as the eggs."

"Oh, Pearl. You're just mad he didn't flirt with you."

As the women bickered over the definition of flirting, the cook glanced at me. He seemed startled to see me there. "You can sit anywhere," he said. "Just pick an open spot."

"I'm actually looking for someone," I told him.

"Who?"

"Daniel Mason." Saying his name gave me a hollow ache. My parents had named my brother Daniel, which told me my dad had loved his brother, even if he didn't speak about him.

The man's brows rose. "And why are you looking for him?"

I immediately knew he was a werecougar like me. The scent was the first clue, and his eyes glowing, just for a second, was another. "You're Daniel Mason, aren't you?"

He moved in closer to me and whispered barely audibly, but with my Shifter senses, I heard him loud and clear. "I go by Buzz these days."

"Who's your new friend, Buzz?" the policewoman asked. Now that she was looking up from her newspaper, I could see she was young.

He flashed a charming smile her way. "Never you mind, Nadine." He gestured to a waitress, a middle-aged woman with sandy-colored hair, wearing a black T-shirt and a blue jean skirt. "Top off her coffee, Freda. Get Nadine's mind on something other than me."

"That'll be a tough 'un, Buzz." Freda laughed. "I don't think Deputy Booth comes here for the cooking."

"More like the cook," the elderly lady with the light strawberry-blonde hair said. She and her friend cackled.

The policewoman's cheeks turned a shade of crimson that flattered her chestnut-brown hair and pale complexion. "Y'all mind your P's and Q's."

Buzz chuckled and shook his head. He turned his attention back to me. "Why is a pretty young thing like you interested in plain ol' me?"

I detected a slight apprehension in his voice.

"If you're Buzz Mason, I'm Lily Mason, and you're my uncle."

The man narrowed his dark-emerald gaze at me. "I think we'd better talk in private."

Keep Reading!

YOU'VE GOT TAIL

PECULIAR MYSTERIES & ROMANCES BOOK 1

Chapter One

SOME PEOPLE JUMP into the deep end of the pool feet first, some head first, but I've always been a traditional belly-flopper. Splashy, messy, and usually painful. Which still didn't explain why I was sitting on the floor of a closed diner, nursing my bruised butt, not to mention my pride, and staring woefully at a naked unconscious man in the middle of Peculiar, Missouri.

My parents are crazy from way back. Maybe that's where I get it from. Seriously, who names a child Ambrosia Sunshine? Two hippies, that's who. They told me when I was old enough to resent the flower child name that they'd thought it was cool at the time, but I personally believe it was the result of one too many 'shrooms. As it is, I've been forced to sit through many painful renditions of "You Are My Sunshine." If I had a dead body for every time I was teased, well, let's just say I'd get an express pass to the electric chair. Although, if I got a sympathetic judge, he'd probably consider my lifetime served.

Maybe my parents' experimentation with drugs is what had made me psychic. (No, I didn't say psychotic. I said *psychic*.) On the other hand, it could also explain why I'm so bad at it.

My ability allows me glimpses, more like screenshots, of the past, present, and future. But, clearly, the visions have *not* been helpful over the years. And the side effects, sheesh. Most of the time I feel a little dizzy when they hit, but every once in a while, it's as if someone has taken a sledgehammer to the inside of my skull. Usually, I can feel one coming on; otherwise driving might be an issue. If only they made medic-alert bracelets for my type of ailment. It certainly hasn't been a gift.

That's why my friendship with Chavvah Trimmel is so important. We'd met at the community college in San Diego. She thought my name was weird and awesome all rolled up into a spring roll. After finding out her family's propensity for strange biblical names, I thought it was a bit of the pot calling the kettle rusty. Chavvah, or Chav, as she likes to be called, was my first best friend. And when she's around me, my psychic mojo kicks up twenty notches. It's as if I can tap into some kind of mystic hotline whenever she's near.

As a matter of fact, the last time I'd gotten a clear vision had been in my dining room back in California. Chav, who'd been renting my spare bedroom at the time, had just turned down the heat on the spaghetti sauce, and I was setting the table. We were having an "I finally dumped the cheating bastard" celebratory dinner. Did I mention I'm a bad psychic? So I hadn't a clue what I was walking in on when I caught my boyfriend of three years having sex with the skank waitress from the coffee shop. On my couch, no less. Jerk. I took his spare key and kicked his ass (and the couch) to the curb.

At dinner that night, when the vision hit me, I'd hit the ground, along with some clattering dishes. I saw a present moment of Chav's parents huddled together, debating whether to call her about her missing brother. Talk about being the bearer of bad news. I didn't blame her for not believing me at first, or the stunned look she gave me when she called her parents, and it turned out to be true. Her brother Judah had dropped off the map.

Chav flew back to Missouri the next day. After a year of searching for him, the local police had pretty much given up on Judah, but by that time, Chav had forgotten about the ocean and fallen in love with the little town of Peculiar. Hell, from her letters and phone calls, I'd kind of fallen in love with the place as well. She'd found a restaurant in the rural town, a real fixer-upper, for the two of us to run. A fifty-fifty partner split.

I wasn't supposed to leave California for another two weeks, and Chav had said she needed to talk to me "in person" before I made the trip, but the text I'd gotten from her had sent me packing in a hurry.

All it said was: *Sunny. I need u.*

After that, every call I'd made to Chav went straight to voice mail. Without any real plan, I jumped into my gas-guzzling Toyota 4X4, which I had purchased explicitly for the move. One thousand six hundred and sixty-two point four miles later, as I drove over a swinging bridge (the only way in and out, I soon discovered) into the quaint little town, my whole body heaved a sigh of relief. I felt strangely wonderful. It was as if someone unzipped my off-the-rack skin and fitted me with a tailored Sunny suit.

The town looked very similar to Mayberry from *The Andy Griffith Show*. Dirt streets, old fashioned shops and houses, white picket fences, and lots of Chevy and Ford pickup trucks. I was a little nervous when my GPS said, "You have arrived," right outside a two-story yellow building on the corner of Third Street and Main.

My heart pounded as I stood outside our restaurant for the first time. I'd always expected some kind of fanfare. Chav waiting to usher me into our future. She'd even named the restaurant for me. Sunny's Outlook. I'd blame allergies for my eyes watering at that moment, but I knew it was a mixture of happiness and sadness all rolled into one big bundle. This was *our* place. Mine and Chav's. And she'd done it up spectacularly.

I smiled at the brightly colored lettering. All the

letters except the big O in Outlook were blue. The O was not an O at all, but a bright orange sun. If it was possible to feel both warm and cold at the same time, I accomplished it.

Where was Chav? I knew in my bones something was wrong. The year we'd spent apart had dulled my psychic ability toward her, so once again I had become inept with crazy flashes that didn't amount to much of anything.

I jiggled the door handle. It wasn't locked, so being the smart, city-savvy girl I am, I decided to let myself in. After all, I owned half the joint, so I wasn't trespassing.

Darkness enclosed the front room except a few areas illuminated by sunlight filtering into the two small windows near the ceiling. They were surrounded by open wooden shutters. Where were the large storefront windows? This place was more dive bar than restaurant. Strange decor choice but my concern for Chav kept me from imagining a complete makeover. I couldn't find a light switch around the door. I should have just gone back out to the truck for a flashlight, but I thought I saw a panel on the wall across the room, and frankly, it was sheer laziness that moved me forward.

I managed to maneuver around the counter, open the panel, and flicked several of the switches at once. The lights came on and when I stepped back to admire my new home lit up—it didn't look half bad; hardwood floors, cute little tables with black-and-white gingham cloth, and a couple of booths with the same checkered design on the benches.

And that's when it happened. My heel caught on something large, and I fell ass-backward to the ground. It didn't take more than a nanosecond to see that I'd tripped over a naked man passed out cold on the floor.

After a startled yelp, heart palpitations, and worry that he'd wake up at any moment and kill me, I reached over and touched him. Just his arm, mind you. He didn't move, but his skin felt warm, and his chest raised and lowered, so I didn't bother to check for a pulse.

Instead, I found myself staring...for several minutes. (Come on. He was naked and lying on his back. Who wouldn't stare?) Dark-brown hair populated his broad chest and led to a happy trail that, well, if the circumstances had been different would have made me very happy indeed. He had thickly muscled thighs and arms, and his face, except for the scruffy five o'clock shadow, looked as if it had been chiseled by Michelangelo. Imagine a better-looking Wolverine (Hugh Jackman's version), but much younger and with a burly lumberjack vibe, and coarse, medium-length walnut-brown hair.

I chewed my lower lip as I took my time pondering the situation—in other words, I wasn't ready to stop staring at the naked man. His hair was near the same hue of brown as my own, when it wasn't dyed blonde, which was never. And mine was shorter with a better haircut. I sighed with regret. I already missed my stylist in California.

Taking a deep breath, I counted backward from ten to pull myself out of the hormonal frenzy going on in my head. The man was hotter than a habanero, but I wasn't looking for a date. I smelled a pungent sweet scent I hadn't noticed before, but frankly I was surprised any of my senses still worked. It was whiskey. Some kind of blended version, if I had to guess.

Great. Just perfect. Burly Hugh looked more and more like a drunk who had crawled into the diner to sleep off a bender.

I found an empty spray bottle by the sink and filled it with water. Positioning myself on the opposite side of the checkout counter (just in case I needed to make a run for it), I leaned over the top and proceeded to spritz the unconscious man. The mist must have been too fine, because other than the rise and fall of his chest, he still didn't move.

Crawling farther up onto the counter, I stretched my arms over the other side, hovering just inches from his face. I pumped the trigger hard three or four times, then screamed and dropped the bottle when his hand shot up and grabbed my wrist. The Neanderthal yanked me completely over the top and onto his naked self. He growled— honest to goodness, I wouldn't lie about such a thing. He growled. The noise started in his chest. I know, because I could feel it in mine, which now crushed against him.

Why hadn't I just left and called the police? It would have been the easy thing to do—the smart thing. His arms were squeezed tight around me, and I became acutely aware of his Mr. Happy pressing against the skin of my thigh.

His eyelids cracked a peep, then he narrowed his gaze. "Who are you?"

"I..." I should be the one asking the damn questions, but the only ones coming to mind were completely inappropriate. Like, where did he work out? How good looking were his parents to create such a fine specimen of man? And did he have a girlfriend?

There was a moment, a very weak moment on my part, where I began to lower my face to his, our lips only centimeters apart.

What the hell am I doing? Where was my head? He could be a serial killer, a rapist, or someone *really* bad, like an Amway salesman. I turned my head away from his.

"Could you let me up, please?"

He squeezed me tighter. "Are you going to answer me?"

Finally, I gulped and squeaked out, "Sunny Haddock."

His left eyebrow rose. "Sunny Haddock?"

"Uh, that would be me. Yes." I'd been in town less than an hour and I was already famous. Well, my name was on the side of the building. "And you would be?"

"Babel Trimmel."

"Chav's baby brother?" I'd heard stories about him,

but I'd imagined him to be terminally twelve. The age he'd been when Chav had left Missouri for the West Coast.

"Chavvie made a big mistake. She shouldn't have asked you out here."

Talk about judging someone before you get the know them. Barely through introductions and he already wanted me out. I've made a bad first impression before, but what the fuck? What didn't he like about me? Although maybe it wasn't about like. Because, by the rise of his hoo-ha against my leg, I could swear he liked me a little.

An unfamiliar flutter twittered in my stomach. It'd been awhile since I'd been so physically attracted to anyone. Babel's nostrils flared with a slight huff. His brows narrowed. His eyes dark with purpose. I felt like Little Red Riding Hood, and Babel filled the role of the Big Bad Wolf intent on eating my goody basket. Oh, if only.

Pull yourself together, Sunny. But it was really hard, along with his arms, his chest, his abs, his...

Holding me tighter, his arms locked around me. He stroked my back with his firm hands. I trembled, fighting back a deep moan. "Please let me up, Babel," I said again.

He froze for a second then relaxed. He unlocked his arms from around me and smiled. "Call me Babe. Every-body does."

To say I scrambled off his body would be a bit of an overstatement. The trembling had left my arms and knees weak, but I managed, albeit slowly. "I don't know you well enough to call you Babe. Sorry." I couldn't keep my eyes off his semi-erect package.

"Could you put some clothes on? I'm feeling a little..."

He propped up on an elbow like a *Playgirl* centerfold and grinned. "Overdressed?"

What an egomaniac! "No. Sheesh." Okay, so maybe I felt a tad overdressed, even in my pink spaghetti-strap shirt dress with black short-shorts and sandals. It was hot in Missouri. Sticky hot. And besides, I'd put in more hours than I care to count at the gym to counterbalance my donut habit, so I deserved to wear those shorts. My exercise routine wasn't all about the donuts. Over a year of no sex, since the dickhead had cheated, and while I'm no sex maniac, that's a long time for someone who had been getting it on the reg.

The "no sex" could also explain why I had such a visceral reaction to this guy. No doubt the man was a hunka-hunka. "Could you quit posing on the floor?" I wagged my finger toward his poker. "And for the love of daisies, put some clothes on before that thing puts out someone's eye."

He had the courtesy to look the tiniest bit embar-rassed. "Nothing personal. It's a purely physical reaction."

"I'm sure you say that to all the girls."

"Sorry, I just meant, well, I'm a guy. You brush against the junk, it goes stiff."

"And here I thought I was special." This line of conversation bordered on hurting my feelings. I know I'm not a beauty queen, but neither am I Medusa. "You can shut up now."

Color rose to his cheeks—those nice fuzzy, chiseled, scruffy, manly cheeks, so perfectly bookending his Roman nose and gorgeous bow lips. And damn it to hell, his teeth were friggin' perfect! He pulled himself up by grabbing the counter, and holy schmoly, the man was tall. If I had to guess, he bordered on 6'5". I'm pretty sure I hated him for being so beautifully handsome.

"I only meant to say..."

I almost offered to buy him a shovel, but he managed to dig his own hole quite deep without any help from me. "I've got it already, jeesh. Not interested, physical reaction, yadda, yadda, yadda. No need to explain yourself further. Besides, I'm not looking for a boyfriend, so doesn't matter. And even if I were, it certainly wouldn't be my best friend's baby brother. We cool?" I didn't wait for him to answer. I waved him off. "Great. Excellent. Awesome even. Now, put on some damn clothes." Why-oh-why was I attracted to crazy?

"Perhaps you could find me a diaper."

Guess he didn't like the "baby" comment. Oh well. Sucks to be him.

He covered himself with his hands. Thank God. However, it didn't stop me from checking out the rest of his body. *Ay Chihuahua!* Damn, it kind of sucked to be me.

I knew from Chav that Babel had moved back to Kansas City where their parents lived after he'd taken a year off from university to look for their brother Judah. What was he still doing here? A horrible thought entered my head. "If you're here, does that mean..."

His face suddenly sobered. "I don't know. Mom and Dad haven't been able to get ahold of her for the last couple of days, so they sent me down to check in. I got here yesterday."

"She texted me a couple of days ago. I haven't been able to get ahold of her since then." I lifted a hand to comfort him, but his nakedness stopped me from breaching the distance. "Babel, we're going to find her." Even if I had to turn over every stump and stone in this backward-ass town.

"Call me Babe. Everyone does."

That was the second time he'd said that to me, but I couldn't call him Babe. No way, no how. Too intimate. Especially since I'd seen him in his birthday suit. "I don't think so."

He chuckled, low and sexy, and everything went right south of my navel. "Sunny,

I'm afraid I've, err...lost my clothes."

"You've got to be kidding me." How did a person go about losing all their damn clothes? "Fine. I'll stay on one side of the counter. You stay on the other. Kapeesh?"

"I understand," he said with a practiced tolerance. It

made me wonder who he'd gotten so much practice with.

He hadn't turned around yet, and part of me felt really sad about it. I'm sure he had a killer butt to go with his killer bod. I was all about the teeth and ass. But there were no complaints about the whole frontal part of him either, so...

"Good. Should I call someone for you? Or do you want to call someone? A girlfriend? Anyone who can bring you some clothes?" Subtle. Not.

"The phone's not working here even if I could call someone."

I noticed he'd didn't say "no girlfriend." Much to my annoyance, I cared. And why was the phone turned off? "Don't you have a cell phone that works?"

He moved his hands, indicating his lack of attire. "No pockets."

In the immortal words of Homer Simpson, *Doh*! I snuck another quick glance at his dangly bits, even more annoyed with myself for not having better self-control. "Great. Fantastic." I waved my hand again and purpose-fully looked away. I had a cell phone out in my truck, and was just about to tell him I'd go get it when he stepped out from behind the counter, still full Monty. "Hey! Keep the mammoth covered."

"Flattering. But there's nothing prehistoric about it." He cocked his eyebrow and smirked.

Bastard.

"Look here, darling." He pointed to his "junk" as he'd

called it and said, "This here is what you call a penis. It's connected to the bladder and the bladder is full. Turn your head if you want, sweetheart, but I'm heading to the john."

"Lovely. And I'm not your darling." I made a show of rolling my eyes and turning away. "I'm going to get my cell phone. I expect you to be standing behind the counter by the time I get back." Now, for the sake of posterity—well, at least for the sake of his posterior—I glanced back as he headed left to the bathroom. Of course, it was sort of hard to notice his ass when I saw the— "Blood..." I whispered.

A pain pierced my temple as my knees buckled beneath me. I dropped to the ground. My peripheral vision narrowed to black. The pounding of blood racing through my arteries swelled loudly in my ears. It was out of beat with my heart.

The thumping of blood stopped, my eyesight began to clear, and I was in Babel's arms.

"Sunny? You okay?" I heard his voice as a muffled echo.

No, I wanted to tell him. I wasn't okay. But my mouth didn't work. A vision came over me. I could sense it like death come knocking. Then I was no longer in Babel's arms. I was a ghost. A spectator.

I was...in a shabby apartment with furniture dating back to the seventies? Had I traveled to the past? It wasn't unheard of for me, but it couldn't be relevant for something in my life now since I hadn't been born until 1974. Or could it? Great.

The powers that be were giving me a psychic reading on my lost Crissy doll. Useless.

I heard a muffled cry, maybe a scream from beyond the front door. I passed through and down the stairs. The noise grew louder. Animalistic growls and snarls. Fear tightened in my stomach.

It's not real, I reminded myself several times as the feral sounds made me shiver.

I couldn't see any creature, but it certainly sounded like someone was getting voraciously attacked. And the room—it looked familiar. Two windows high up on the far wall spilled moonlight across the floor to...the counter? This was the restaurant. The noise continued, loud, animalistic, with grunting, groaning, and a masculine "ah!" Oh. Oh no.

If I'd really been there, I'd have run, but the vision took me closer to the scene of the crime. On the floor, behind the counter, a gorgeous woman with long dark hair, golden eyes, and even in the bad lighting, a body I'd give my right tit for, straddled the very naked and very sexy Babel Trimmel. I wanted to gouge out my eyes. Where was a hot poker salesman when you needed him?

The woman threw her head back and laughed. "You were fantastic, Babe. As always."

He smiled, his eyes rolling back a little. Coming up on his elbows, he leaned his left shoulder forward and looked behind. "You've got to do something about those fingernails."

"Just marking my territory."

Holy smack, the blood on the floor had happened during sexcapades? Yikes.

"I'm not your territory, Sheila."

The woman, Sheila apparently, picked up a bottle of Canadian Mist from the floor beside them, took a swig, then dumped some of the amber liquid down his large chest. No wonder the place reeked.

Babel shook his head and gave her thigh a light slap. "It's time to go, Sheila. I've got to get the place cleaned up."

"You sure you don't want to move here?" She licked his nipple. "I've sure missed you."

He sighed. The sigh sounded like it'd been one that he'd perfected over and over for this very argument. "It's not this town or you. I've got a real life out there." *He said "there" as though he was talking about an alien planet. "I'm going to find my sister, then get back to it."*

"And what if you don't find her?" Sheila asked. "You never found Judah."

Babel's eyes narrowed. "Not an option," he said. Then added, "I'm finding her, and after, getting the heck out of this town. It's brought nothing but bad luck for my family."

"Sorry," she said, as if she wasn't sorry, an evil smile playing on her lips. Okay, so maybe more mischievous than evil, but it was my vision, I could use whatever adjectives I liked. "But you know that answer pisses me off."

Before he could blink, she whacked him super hard across the temple with the bottle of blended whiskey, and Babel was out like a light.

"Bastard," Sheila muttered. Which I understood, because it had been my sentiment exactly.

She dressed quickly, gathered up Babel's clothes, and

walked into the kitchen area. It was small, but nice. I hadn't had a chance to see it yet, so it was like my very own psychic tour. She opened the walk-in freezer and chucked the jeans, boots, socks, and T-shirt inside. No underwear. Huh. I'd file that nugget away for later.

My vision stopped with her slamming the front door, and suddenly I was back, looking up from the floor at the towering and still very naked Babel. "Ow." My head, my back, my butt—everything hurt. "Did you drop me?"

"What the hell just happened?" He looked a little freaked out.

I got up on my elbows and rubbed the back of my skull. "Did you drop me on the ground?"

"You were having a seizure or something. I laid you on the floor." He was definitely freaked. "If I'd had a phone I'd have called for the doc, but..."

"I'm fine now. You can stop worrying." I moved my feet off the chair Babel had propped them up on.

"I'm sorry. I'm squeamish about blood."

Which wasn't a complete lie. Blood tended to bring on funky psychic mojo that left me drained and pained. Although, I'll admit, these visions had been much stronger than normal. Apparently, Chavvah wasn't the only Trimmel who put my psychic stuff on speed dial.

"I'm getting that about you." At least he sounded less upset.

I closed my eyes. "Why would you let someone do that to your back?"

"That's a story for another day, darlin'."

Yeah, I knew the story. Not so sure I wanted the blow-by-blow again. I felt his arms go under me, and I opened my eyes, staring into the deep abyss of his gorgeous, Midwest baby blues.

I let him carry me upstairs to the apartment. I'm not a small woman, but he held me like I weighed next to nothing, which made me think kindlier of him. With my arms around his shoulders, I could smell an unidentifiable musk and spice to his skin. He sat me down on a couch—the scent went from musky to musty—then he went into another room. I heard water running in the sink. More than a whisper of regret passed through me. I barely knew the man and I missed being in his arms. I looked around the living room.

This was the seventies place where my vision had started. The retro decor lacked any sophistication that could've made the space sensational. I knew this had been where Judah lived when he'd been in town. He'd rented this building before his disappearance, and Chav had used our stake to purchase it during her search for him. His vanishing had hit her hard.

Chav told me once that she hadn't agreed with her oldest brother's "lifestyle choice," but she respected him. I'd asked her what she meant, but she had shaken her head, unwilling to elaborate. I knew it wasn't as simple as him being gay or anything like that, because Chav, like myself, was socially liberal. Hell, she'd have started her own PFLAG (Parents, Families, and Friends of Lesbians and Gays) in Peculiar if that had been the case. No. There was something else she hadn't approved of.

I heard the water turn off in the kitchen. Babel returned and proceeded to wipe my face and neck with a cool cloth.

"There now, all better." For a second, he sounded like my father. Which totally squicked me, considering the hard-core fantasies I had about him. He put the washcloth in my hand and patted my shoulder. "I'm going to jump in the shower real quick. I'll be back in a few."

Part of me wanted to watch him walk away strictly for the view, but since that part seemed to have done gone and lost its damn mind, I waited until I heard water running before looking in his direction.

He'd left the bathroom door open. Perv.

I couldn't believe it, less than an hour in a new town and I'd witnessed a *Red Shoe Diary* moment, and the star was lathering up less than ten feet away. I would've been downright disgusted by the whole morning if I hadn't been so preoccupied with thoughts of slippery suds sliding along his perfectly formed pecs. (Now I understand how bad porn gets started. Bow chick-a bow-wow.)

I will not go stare at the naked man. I repeated this mantra in my head over and over as I ran down the stairs to the kitchen.

Grabbing his clothes from the freezer, I contemplated where they'd been and how they got there as I carried them back upstairs. They were cold and held the scent of sweat, but at least he'd have something to put on so he could go away. I placed them on the couch, and dear Lord, it was a really ugly couch. It would be the first piece of furniture to go when Chav and I started fixing the place up. And with that thought, I went downstairs to wait for him.

Fifteen minutes later, the light flickered on in the stairwell. Babel's arms and face glistened with dewy goodness as he walked down the steps. He rubbed a tea towel, barely big enough to dry a fish's butt, against his loose mane of wet hair. His blue T-shirt clung to his chest. Water soaking through the fabric made spots the color of midnight.

He must have felt me staring, because he dropped his arm to his side and looked at me. "Where'd you find my clothes?"

"The freezer." I wrapped my knuckle on the counter. "Guess you can go home now."

"Guess so." He shrugged as he stretched his body to tuck in his shirt. "But we should probably talk."

"I'm in no mood." *For talk.* Damn, he was super-fine.

"Well, you kind of need to get in the mood." He shook his hair out, droplets spraying out around him. It began to feel like a bad (or really good, depending on who you asked) shampoo commercial. "There's been a mistake. My sister should've never invited you out here, Sunny."

"You've said that already, but unfortunately for you, my name's on the property, same as hers, all legal and binding. I'm staying. Period. End of discussion. Besides, I'm not going anywhere until I find Chav."

Babel chewed his lower lip and narrowed his eyes at me. "I don't think you understand the situation."

"Oh, I think I do. You don't like me. Fine. I get that."

"It's a might more complicated than that." He scratched at his five o'clock shadow.

I resisted the temptation to offer him a hand. "Why do you care, anyway? Don't you have a *real* life you want to get back to? You seem awfully concerned for a guy who isn't even sticking around."

"And what makes you think that?" Babel asked.

"Uh..." Fair question. I couldn't exactly tell him that I'd heard him tell his cuh-razy lover in a vision. "Well, you didn't exactly stick around after the search was called off for Judah."

A pained expression crossed his face. I instantly regretted being such an ass. It was a low blow, and petty even.

"I stayed for as long as I could stand it." He shook his head. "I'm not meant for this place, Sunny. And neither are you."

Another twinge. "It doesn't matter." We would find Chavvah, then he would be gone. "Have you heard anything? Are the police searching for her?"

"No and yes. I haven't heard from Chavvie, but

Sheriff Taylor isn't giving up." He flicked his thumbnail against his ring fingernail. "Not yet, anyways."

"She'll show up, Babel. I just know it." But I didn't know it. In my heart, I believed she was alive, and not because of any vision. "She's my best friend. I'd feel it if she was gone. Now, go on back to wherever you're staying..." Oh, crap. Maybe he'd been staying here. "You do have another place to stay don't you?"

Babel nodded once. "I've been staying at Chavvie's cabin down by the lake."

"Good," I whispered. I'd want to check out her place later for clues to what happened. "It's been a long drive for me, and I need a nap so I can figure out what I have to do next to find her."

He shook his head as if he was having an argument with himself. "I'll be back in a couple of hours with some cleaning supplies and get the floor behind the counter scrubbed."

I didn't want to talk anymore. I wanted to get my bags out of the truck. I'd hassle with unpacking the U-Haul later, but the bags were a must. I needed something personal, something of mine in this place. I held out my hand. "That's a nice offer. I can manage. Thanks."

Babel took my hand, and gave me a tight-lipped smile. "You don't handle blood very well. After I clean it up, maybe we can compare notes about Chavvie."

I nodded, afraid that if I spoke the dams would open

and I wouldn't be able to stop the tears. Then I heard a voice like a whisper in my ear.

Save her.

Babel let go of my hand. "I'll be back." The way he said it sounded more like a threat than a promise. As he walked out the front door, he added, "You've got an audience."

Get this book from your favorite eTailer!

PARANORMAL MYSTERIES & ROMANCES

BY RENEE GEORGE

Nora Black Midlife Psychic Mysteries

Sense & Scent Ability (Book 1)

For Whom the Smell Tolls (Book 2)

War of the Noses (Book 3)

Aroma With A View (Book 4)

Spice and Prejudice (Book 5)

Age of Inno-Scents (Book 6)

Aroma Holiday (Book 7)

Vapes of Wrath (Book 8)

The Scented Cipher (Book 9)

Grimoires of a Middle-aged Witch

Earth Spells Are Easy (Book 1)

Spell On Fire (Book 2)

When the Spells Blows (Book 3)

Spell Over Troubled Water (Book 4)

Ghost in the Spell (Book 5)

Destiny of a Middle-aged Witch

Burning Djinn of Fire (Book 1)

Djinn Bottle Blues (Book 2)

Stand By Your Djinn (Book 3)

Peculiar Mysteries & Romances

You've Got Tail (Book 1)

My Furry Valentine (Book 2)

Thank You For Not Shifting (Book 3)

My Hairy Halloween (Book 4)

In the Midnight Howl (Book 5)

Furred Lines (Book 6)

My Wolfy Wedding (Book 7)

Who Let The Wolves Out? (Book 8)

My Thanksgiving Faux Paw (Book 9)

Witchin' Impossible Paranormal Mysteries

Witchin' Impossible (Book 1)

Rogue Coven (Book 2)

Familiar Protocol (Booke 3)

Mr & Mrs. Shift (Book 4)

FurOut (Book 5)

Barkside of the Moon Paranormal Mysteries

Pit Perfect Murder (Book 1)

Murder & The Money Pit (Book 2)

The Pit List Murders (Book 3)

Pit & Miss Murder (Book 4)

The Prune Pit Murder (Book 5)

Two Pits and A Little Murder (Book 6)

Pits and Pieces of Murder (Book 7)

Pittie Party Murder (Book 8)

Hex Drive

Hex Me, Baby, One More Time (Book 1)

Oops, I Hexed It Again (Book 2)

I Want Your Hex (Book 3)

Hex Me With Your Best Shot (Book 4)

Hex Me All Night Long (Book 5)

ABOUT THE AUTHOR

I am a USA Today Bestselling author who writes paranormal mysteries and romances because I love all things whodunit, Otherworldly, and weird. Also, I wish my pittie, the adorable Kona Princess Warrior and my two cats Ash and Simon could talk. Or at least be more like Scooby-Doo and help me unmask villains at the haunted house up the street.

When I'm not writing about mystery-solving were-cougars or the adventures of a hapless psychic living among shapeshifters, I am preyed upon by stray kittens who end up living in my house because I can't say no to those sweet, furry faces. (Someone stop telling them where I live!)

I live in Mid-Missouri with my family and I spend my non-writing time doing really cool stuff...like watching TV and cleaning up dog poop

Follow Renee!
Bookbub
Renee's Rebel Readers FB Group
Newsletter

PRAISE FOR RENEE GEORGE

"Sense and Scent Ability by Renee George is a delightfully funny, smart, full of excitement, up-all-night fantastic read! I couldn't put it down. The latest installment in the Paranormal Women's Fiction movement, knocks it out of the park. Do yourself a favor and grab a copy today!"

— —ROBYN PETERMAN NYT
BESTSELLING AUTHOR

"I'm loving the Paranormal Women's Fiction genre! Renee George's humor shines when a woman of a certain age sniffs out the bad guy and saves her bestie. Funny, strong female friendships rule!"

— -- MICHELLE M. PILLOW, NYT & USAT
BESTSELLING AUTHOR

"I smell a winner with Renee George's new book, Sense & Scent Ability! The heroine proves that being over fifty doesn't have to stink, even if her psychic visions do."

— -- MANDY M. ROTH, NY TIMES
BESTSELLING AUTHOR

"Sense & Scent Ability is everything! Nora Black is sassy, smart, and her smell-o-vision is scent-sational. I can't wait for the next Nora book!

— —MICHELE FREEMAN, *AUTHOR OF HOMETOWN HOMICIDE, A SHERIFF BLUE HAYES MYSTERY*